FREEWAY

An Integrated Course in Communicative English

STUDENT BOOK 3

Cheryl Pavlik

Anna Stumpfhauser de Hernandez

Contents

Contents

At the Start

1. ▭ Look at the picture and listen to the conversation. Which people are talking?

2. Now answer the questions.
a. Where did the man and woman go on their vacation?
b. How long did they stay there?
c. What did they do there?
d. Did they have a good vacation?
e. When are they going back?

1 Verb Review

Ray is talking to his wife, Miranda, on his cellular phone. Look at the picture and complete the conversation. Use the verbs from the box.

listen wake up pay have run sleep
fight talk tell do eat read

RAY: How's everything at home, Miranda?
MIRANDA: Fine, Ray. How about you?
RAY: I ¹..... a headache. There are these two little kids on the bus. They ²..... up and down the aisle, and now they ³..... about something, I don't know what.
MIRANDA: Maybe you should ⁴..... them to calm down.
RAY: Well, I did, but they ⁵..... any attention to me.
          ₙₒₜ
MIRANDA: What about their parents?
RAY: Oh, they ⁶..... .
MIRANDA: And the bus driver?
RAY: He also ⁷..... them to be quiet, but they ⁸..... .
          ₙₒₜ
MIRANDA: And what about the other people on the bus? What ⁹..... they ..... ?
RAY: About the children? Nothing. The woman next to me ¹⁰..... a sandwich, the people at the front ¹¹..... , one of the boys in front of me ¹²..... to music, the other one ¹³..... .
MIRANDA: That's too bad, Ray.
RAY: Well, never mind. There's only one solution. I have to ¹⁴..... their parents.
MIRANDA: Good luck, Ray. See you soon.
RAY: Bye, Miranda.

2 Comparatives and Superlatives

The two boys on the bus are fighting about their toy cars. Complete the conversation using the correct adjective forms.

FIRST BOY: My car is ¹..... than yours.
_{big}

SECOND BOY: Well, maybe, but mine is ²..... .
_{fast}

FIRST BOY: It is not! My car is ³..... car in the
_{fast}
whole world.

SECOND BOY: It can't be. My car has ⁴..... engine
_{powerful}
in the world, so it has to be ⁵.....,
_{fast}
too.

FIRST BOY: Well, mine was ⁶..... than yours, so
_{expensive}
that means it's ⁷..... .
_{good}

SECOND BOY: It does not!

FIRST BOY: Does too!

3 Find the Errors

Rewrite the sentences correctly.
a. I don't want some salad, thank you.
b. Please ask she to call me.
c. We working on our thesis.
d. I going to have an exam tomorrow.
e. What is she write?
f. He has a teethache.
g. What movie are they going see?
h. We didn't went to the bookstore yesterday.

4 Talk in Pairs

1. Choose one of the people on the bus. Decide on the following information.
a. their name
b. their occupation
c. where they live
d. what they were doing before they got on the bus
e. where they are going
f. what they are going to do

2. Ask your partner questions about the person he or she chose.

5 Writing

1. Write a paragraph about your partner's person. Read your paragraph to the class.

2. Write descriptions of three of these people from the bus.

3. Put the words in order to make sentences.
a. you/do/your/do/have/homework/to/now/?
b. to/goes/on/Friday/movies/Susie/night/the/always/.
c. children/get/they/their/angry/never/with/.

The Case of the Suspicious Suicide

Jim Rogers, one of the owners of Rogers and Wilson, was still working at 7 o'clock at night. The company was in trouble. Someone was stealing money and he had to find out who it was!

His partner, Paul Wilson, was writing a letter in his office.

The only other person in the building was a secretary, Marcy O'Connor. At 7:15 she was typing some letters when Paul Wilson called her into his office. He asked her to go out to mail a letter.

Marcy O'Connor came back after 10 minutes. She and Paul Wilson were looking at some files when suddenly they heard a shot from Jim Rogers' office.

They ran to his door. It was locked! Marcy found the key in her desk. They unlocked the office door and went in. There was Jim Rogers, dead with a bullet wound in his head. Marcy O'Connor immediately called the police and reported a suicide.

When the police arrived, they examined Jim Rogers' office carefully. They found several clues. There was no suicide note, but they found a signed check and some file folders on the desk. The gun was lying on the floor next to Jim Rogers' hand. The office seemed very warm. A small heater was on, even though it was a warm night. Near the heater they discovered a small piece of rubbery plastic.

"Well, I know one thing for sure," said the police detective. "This was a homicide, not a suicide!"

At the Start

1. Look through the story and find the name of the man in the pictures.

2. Read the story. Does the detective think the man killed himself? Do you agree?

Dictionary Work `DICT`

1. Look up these words in the dictionary. How are they pronounced?
suicide   wound   suspicious   trouble   signed
examined   dead   typing

Take turns saying the words aloud with a partner. Did you say them correctly? If you disagree, ask your teacher.

2. Look up the word *suspicious*. Which definition, 1 or 2, is the one used in the story?

3. Look up the word *wound*. Which two parts of speech can it be? Check the two pronunciations with your partner. Which definition is the one used in the story?

2 Spotlight

1. Study the structures below.

They **found** the key, **unlocked** the door and **went** in.

They **were looking** at some files when they **heard** a gunshot.

2. Complete these rules about the formation and use of the past continuous and the simple past.
a. The past continuous is formed with the ..... tense of ..... followed by the verb + ...
b. To show actions that happened one after another like this: **x x x**, you use the ..... tense.
c. To show that one action happened while another was in progress, like this: **<----x-->**, you use the ..... tense for the action in progress, and the ..... tense for the new or interrupting action.

3. Read these sentences. Decide if they follow rule b or c above.
a. I was cooking dinner when the lights went off.
b. I cooked dinner and then the lights went off.
c. The telephone rang as she was getting out of bed.
d. She got out of bed when the telephone rang.

3 Listening

1. 📼 Listen to the rest of *The Case of the Suspicious Suicide* and take notes.

2. Now write a paragraph about who killed Jim Rogers and how.

4 Practice

Complete the paragraph with the simple past or past continuous.

One day when Tom ¹..... to work he ²..... an
⎣drive⎦   ⎣have⎦
accident. He ³..... a corner when a big dog ⁴.....
         ⎣turn⎦   ⎣run⎦
in front of his car. Tom quickly ⁵..... on the
                              ⎣step⎦
brake and ⁶..... but the car behind him ⁷..... too
      ⎣stop⎦   ⎣go⎦
fast. The driver couldn't stop. He ⁸..... Tom's car.
                               ⎣hit⎦
No one ⁹..... hurt but both cars were damaged.
   ⎣be⎦
The men ¹⁰..... their cars in the street and ¹¹..... to
     ⎣leave⎦   ⎣go⎦
call the police. While they ¹²..... the police,
                        ⎣call⎦
someone ¹³..... Tom's car stereo!
     ⎣steal⎦

5 Talk in Pairs

1. With your partner look at the pictures and make up a story. Try to use the past continuous and the simple past tense.

2. Tell your story to your class.

Before You Read

Look at the advertisement. This is probably:
a. a magazine ad.   c. a TV commercial.
b. a billboard.

DOLE USES ONLY THE BEST PART OF THE PINEAPPLE SO YOUR SALADS WILL TASTE AS GOOD AS THIS ONE LOOKS

FREE RECIPE BOOKLET. SEND STAMPED SELF-ADDRESSED ENVELOPE TO DOLE, P.O.BOX 7758, SAN FRANCISCO, CALIFORNIA 94120.

DOLE USES ONLY THE JUICIEST, SWEETEST PART OF THE FRESH PINEAPPLE – PACKED IN ITS OWN JUICE. NO SUGAR ADDED.

1 Reading

1. Read the ad and answer the following questions TRUE or FALSE.
a. This pineapple has only the natural sugar from pineapple.
b. This pineapple is packed in orange juice.
c. Dole doesn't use the whole pineapple.
d. You don't have to pay to get this recipe.

2. The purpose of this ad is to convince you to:
a. eat something.
b. buy Dole pineapple.
c. make salads.

3. Do you think this ad achieves its purpose? Why or why not?

2 Spotlight

1. Look at the following diagrams.

a. 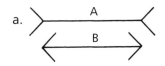   b. 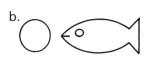   c.

a. Does line A look **as long as** line B?
b. Is the eye of the fish **as round as** the circle?
c. Is circle A **as big as** circle B?

2. Read the ad and find a sentence with *as...as*.

3. Complete the following sentence.
We use (not) ..... + adjective + ... when we want to show that two things are the same (or not).

4. Which of the following sentences mean the same?
a. Dark chocolate is not as good as light chocolate.
b. Light chocolate is better than dark chocolate.
c. Dark chocolate is better than light chocolate.
d. Light chocolate is as good as dark chocolate.

3 Listening

1. Read the following questions.

a. Where is the sale?

b. When is the sale?

c. What is for sale?

d. What is on sale?

e. Does everything have the same discount?

f. Are the shoes on sale the newest style or last year's style?

g. Why do they say that this is "the hottest" sale?

2. Now listen to the radio commercial and answer the questions.

4 Talk in Pairs or Groups

1. What attracts your attention to ads? Do you think people buy products because of ads?

2. Do you watch TV commercials? Describe a TV commercial that you remember. Why do you remember it?

3. What kind of advertising do you remember the most? TV, radio, newspapers, magazines? Why?

4. Do you think ads tell the truth? Why or why not?

5. What things do you think should not be advertised?

5 Writing   DICT

1. Find the superlative of the following adjectives in the ad and complete the chart. Check in your dictionary for the meaning of any words you don't know.

Adjective	Superlative
sweet	
juicy	
good	
delicious	the most delicious

2. Complete the sentences with the correct superlative form.

a. I thought this last exam was ..... .
_{difficult}

b. Your suitcase is ..... of them all. What did you put in it?
_{heavy}

c. Who has ..... handwriting in this class?
_{neat}

d. Why do you always choose ..... clothes?
_{expensive}

e. My sister is ..... person I know. She is nice to everybody.
_{friendly}

3. There are ads for almost everything. Some common products in ads are: clothes, food, cars and beauty products. Choose one of these products and make up your own ad or commercial.

At the Start

1. Do you keep a diary? Would you let anyone read it?

2. 🔲 Listen to this conversation between Fran and Jerry.

3. Now answer the questions.
a. What is Fran and Jerry's relationship?
b. How long ago did they meet?
c. What is Jerry reading?

1 Dictionary Work `DICT`

1. Look up these words and phrases.
creep   fall in love   love at first sight
lovesick   lover   loving

Use each word or phrase in a sentence.

2. Look up these words.
private   handsome   diary

Take turns saying the words with a partner to check your pronunciation. Which word has three syllables? Which word has a silent consonant?

2 Spotlight

1. Study the structures below.

A: This **isn't** our anniversary, **is it?**
B: No, it's not. (Yes, it is.)

A: She **remembers,** **doesn't she?**
B: Yes, she does. (No, she doesn't.)

A: It **was** love at first sight, **wasn't it?**
B: Yes, it was. (No, it wasn't.)

A: You **didn't** read my diary, **did you?**
B: No, I didn't. (Yes, I did.)

2. Complete the following rules about tag questions.
a. If the statement is positive, the tag question is ..... and the response is expected to be ..... .
b. If the statement is negative, the tag question is ..... and the response is expected to be ..... .

3. Look at the statements and complete the tag questions.

a. She went, ... ?
b. You're not a student, ... ?
c. He's going, ... ?
d. They didn't see you, ... ?

3 Pronunciation

1. 🔲 Tag questions have two different tunes. Listen to the following examples.

a. Tag questions go down when you're SURE the statement is true:

You didn't like your gift, did you?
He doesn't speak English, does he?
She'll forget my birthday, won't she?

b. Tag questions go up when you are NOT SURE if the statement is true:

You didn't lose your keys, did you?
We aren't late, are we?
I can come in now, can't I?

2. 🔲 Listen and say if the tag questions go up or down.

a. She wants to go, doesn't she?
b. They don't need $2000, do they?
c. I didn't need all those clothes, did I?
d. You had a wonderful time, didn't you?
e. We aren't leaving today, are we?

Listen again and repeat. What do you think the response would be and why?

4 Listening

🔲 Read the questions, then listen to the rest of the conversation between Fran and Jerry and answer them.

a. How did Fran describe the man she met?
b. What was his name?
c. Did she dance with Jerry?
d. How did she describe Jerry?
e. Who did she leave with?
f. When did Jerry fall in love with Fran?
g. When did Fran fall in love with Jerry?

5 Practice

1. Complete the conversations.

a. A: You forgot to stop at the store, ... ?
   B: Sorry. I was talking to Phil in the car and I drove right by.
b. A: Your students left you a package. Open it.
   B: They didn't buy me a present, ... ?
c. A: Jim's taking tomorrow off. It's July 4th, American Independence Day.
   B: He's not American, ... ?
d. A: I'll meet you on the corner at six. Look for a red Volkswagen.
   B: But you have a Honda, ... ?

2. Look at the pictures. What do you think the people are saying?

6 Talk in Pairs

Think of three things about another student in class that you think you know. Check the information by asking your partner tag questions.
Example:
A: *You're studying engineering, aren't you?*
B: *No, I'm not. I'm studying law.*

A: *You aren't from Mexico, are you?*
B: *No, I'm not. I'm from Venezuela.*

At the Start

1. Bill and Marcy's car won't start. They have to walk 20 miles. What should they take with them?

2. 🔊 Now listen to their conversation. What things are they going to take?

1 Dictionary Work DICT

1. What is the pronunciation of *gh* in these words?
enough   rough   tough   laugh

2. What is the pronunciation of *ph* in these words?
pharmacy   telephone   phrase

3. Take turns saying the words aloud to your partner. Do you agree on the pronunciations? If not, ask your teacher.

2 Spotlight

1. Study the following structures.

It's **too big** to carry.   It's **not small enough** to carry.
It's **not too big** to carry.   It's **small enough** to carry.
It's **too far** to walk.   It's **not close enough** to walk.
It's **not too far** to walk.   It's **close enough** to walk.

2. Look at the picture and complete the sentences.
a. The elephant is ..... to get into the phone booth.
b. The elephant isn't ..... to get into the phone booth.
c. The man is ..... to get into the phone booth.
d. The man isn't ..... to get into the phone booth.

3 Practice

1. Look at the people and make sentences from the following phrases with *(not) too old/young* and *(not) old/young enough*.

Example: *to vote*
Erik is too young to vote. Erik is not old enough to vote.

a. to go to school
b. to drive a car
c. to get married
d. to retire
e. to leave school

Cindy

Erik

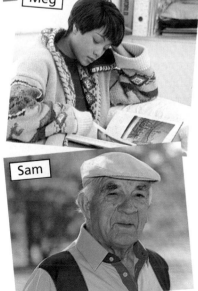
Meg

Sam

2. Use the cues and the adjectives to make as many statements as you can with *too* or *enough*.

tall   slow   short   fast   heavy   high   small   low   light

a.   She is/isn't ..... .
     The car is/isn't ..... .

b.   He is/isn't ..... .
     The light is/isn't ..... .

c.   She is/isn't ..... .
     The books are/aren't ..... .

d.   He drives/doesn't drive
     ..... .

4 Talk in Groups

You are planning to go camping in the mountains with some friends. Look at the picture and choose the three most important things for each person to take and the six most important things for the group to take.

campstove   sleeping bag   tent   hiking boots   gas canister
matches   plates   canned soda   radio   raincoat   pot   silverware
football   bathing suit   first aid kit   canned soup   crackers
candy bars   soap   pillow   compass   map

Before You Read

1. Glance through the article. It is mainly about:
a. TV.
b. a child.
c. a magician.

2. Magicians do:
a. bad things.
b. tricks.
c. common things.

1 Reading

1. Read the article.

2. Which of the following would be a good title?
a. The Magic of David Copperfield
b. How to do Magic
c. Famous Magicians

3. Now answer these questions TRUE or FALSE.
a. David Copperfield performs only in the U.S.
b. David Copperfield learned to do his magic tricks at school.
c. David Copperfield likes to buy clothes.
d. David Copperfield works in Las Vegas every year.

4. Put the following events in order.
a. He was a ventriloquist.
b. He started working on TV.
c. He made a TV program.
d. He acted in a play.
e. He spent Saturdays in a magic shop.

Now you see it – now you don't. This happens all the time around David Copperfield, even when the "it" is the Statue of Liberty in New York harbor. However, he not only makes things disappear. He also walks through the Great Wall of China, goes over Niagara Falls and appears to fly. In all his acts, he takes his audience on unbelievable trips through the world of magic.

David Copperfield's original name was David Kotkin, and as a child, he was skinny and shy. He did not always want to be a magician. First, he wanted to be a ventriloquist, but he discovered that he was not very good at "throwing his voice." Then, he tried magic. He spent every Saturday at a magic shop in New York, where he made friends with magicians and learned some tricks. When he was 17, he got the main part in the play, *The Magic Man*. Next, Copperfield made a TV program, and after that, he was hired by the American TV company, CBS. He still works for CBS, but he also performs on tours throughout the country, and he works in Las Vegas 10 weeks of the year.

Copperfield loves his work, and he has little time for anything else, even for buying clothes. He doesn't even know his own size, because someone else always buys his clothes for him. Of course, this is not a difficult job, because his wardrobe consists of 50 pairs of black Levi jeans.

Copperfield enjoys creating new tricks that continue to fascinate people of all ages and nationalities.

2 Vocabulary Building DICT

1. Use your dictionary to complete the table.

Nouns	
Area of work/study	**Person**
magic	magician
electricity	electrician
music	
politics	
pediatrics	
chemistry	chemist
ventriloquism	ventriloquist
pharmacy	
biology	
psychology	
therapy	

2. Fill in the blanks with one of the words above.

a. I'd like to know how ..... can throw their voices.

b. Something is wrong with the lights. I'm going to call the ..... .

c. ..... is a very interesting subject. It's nice to understand how living things function.

d. I don't think I got a good grade in ..... . There are too many theories about human behavior.

e. I don't want to be a ..... . Imagine having to work in a drugstore all day!

3 Talk in Pairs or Groups

Tell a classmate about the life of somebody you admire. Talk about what the person did, and why they are special. Take notes about the person your partner describes.

4 Writing

1. Look at the sentences in the box.

First, he wanted to become a ventriloquist.
Then, he tried magic.
Next, he acted in a play.
After that, he worked in a TV special.
Finally, he was hired by CBS.

2. Which words are important in showing the order, or sequence, of the events?

3. What kind of punctuation follows these words?

4. Read the article about David Copperfield again. Now, use your notes to write a biography about the person your partner described. Follow this pattern:

Paragraph 1: Who is this person? What is special about him/her?

Paragraph 2: Where was he/she born? What was interesting or admirable about his/her childhood, teenage years and/or adult years?

At the Start

1. Do you ever ask for advice? Would you ask someone that you didn't know?

2. 🔲 Listen to the following radio advice show and answer these questions.
a. What's Terry's girlfriend's name?
b. What does Terry's girlfriend do that he doesn't like?
c. What does Dr. Weston suggest?
d. Does Terry think that's a good idea? Why or why not?

1 Dictionary Work DICT

1. Look in the dictionary. Find the words to complete the table.

Verbs	Adjectives	Nouns
.....	married	.....
.....	divorced	.....
	widowed	.....

2. Look up these phrases in the dictionary. Use each one in a sentence.
drive (someone) crazy
break up with (someone)
show up (somewhere)

3. Look up these words in the dictionary. What parts of speech are they?
advice advisor advise

2 Spotlight

1. Study these modals.

might/might not (probability)
    She **might** get angry.
    She **might not** show up for the wedding.

can/can't (ability)
    You **can** explain to her.
    I **can't** talk to her now.

will/won't (promise)
    We'**ll** have to give back the presents.
    I **won't** forget.

should/shouldn't (advisability)
    Maybe you **should** leave her.
    She **shouldn't** be so sensitive.

2. Look at these pairs of sentences. How are they different?
a. She won't work.   She can't work.
b. I might stay.   I should stay.
c. They will do the   They should do the
   work.   work.
d. You shouldn't go.   You can't go.
e. He might not study.   He won't study.
f. We can go to a   We might go to a
   restaurant.   restaurant.

3 Practice

Read the situations and complete the sentences.

1. Bob and his wife Carla don't get along well. They argue every day. They both want to get divorced, but they have four young children.
a. Bob and Carla should ..... .
b. Bob and Carla shouldn't ..... .
c. The children will ..... .
d. The children won't ..... .

2. Karen wants to leave school. She's only 15. It's against the law to leave school before you are 16.
a. Karen can't ..... .
b. Karen's parents should ..... .
c. Karen should ..... .
d. Karen might ..... .

3. Brad wants a motorcycle. Brad's parents think it's very dangerous. They won't let him buy a motorcycle.
a. Brad can't ..... .
b. Brad might not ..... .
c. Brad's parents will ..... .
d. Brad's parents won't ..... .

4 Listening

1. 🔊 Listen to the conversation between a teenaged boy and his mother. What does he want to do? Does she agree?

2. What does she think might happen?

5 Pronunciation

🔊 Listen to these sentences. Notice how the ending /t/ sound is lost before another consonant.
a. He might go.
b. It doesn't make sense.
c. She won't stay.
d. You might not study.
e. They shouldn't drive.

Now listen again and repeat the sentences.

6 Talk in Pairs

1. Complete these sentences with your partner.
a. A good friend should ..... .
b. A good friend shouldn't ..... .
c. A good friend might ..... .
d. A good friend might not ..... .
e. A good friend will ..... .
f. A good friend won't ..... .
g. A good friend can ..... .
h. A good friend can't ..... .

2. Now share your ideas with your class.

At the Start

1. Do you grow plants? What kind of plants do you grow?

2.  In California, Tom Borchard is known as Mr. October and instead of a "green thumb," people say that he has an "orange thumb." Listen to this interview with Mr. Borchard and you will see why.

3. Now answer these questions.
a. Why do people say Tom Borchard has an "orange thumb"? What does he grow?
b. How big was the largest one?

1 Dictionary Work `DICT`

1. Look up the pronunciation of *s* in these words:
unusual   sure   measure   sugar

Check your pronunciation with a partner.

2. Look up the pronunciation of *gh* in these words:
neighbor   weigh

3. Look back at the pronunciation of *gh* in Unit 4. Complete this statement:
gh can be pronounced like ..... or it is ..... .

2 Spotlight

1. Study the structures below.

Have you **ever entered** a competition before?
Yes, I **have**.
No, I **haven't**.

Has he **ever won** any prizes?
Yes, he **has won** prizes before.
No, he **never has**.

Have you **ever jumped** from a plane before?
Yes, I **have**.
No, I've **never jumped** from a plane.

2. *Have you ever...* refers to
a. any time in your life.
b. a particular time in your life.

3 Listening

1. 📼 Listen to this poem and complete it.

Question Box

Have you [1]..... jumped out of a plane?
Have you ever traveled in [2]..... ?
[3]..... you ever [4]..... a mountain?
Have you [5]..... swum in a [6]..... ?
Have you ever [7]..... a horse?

Now, wait a [8]..... . Of course
[9]..... never jumped out of a plane,
And I've [10]..... traveled in Spain,
I [11]..... care about [12]..... mountains,
And who ever [13]..... of swimming [14].....
    fountains,
But I've [15]..... lots of things too,
[16]..... I'll bet you never [17]..... .

2. Write your own four line poem of *have you ever...*
questions

4 Practice

Complete the following conversation using the cues.

JOE: How's it going, Walt?

WALT: I'm not sure. My car isn't working and I'm trying to fix it,
but...

JOE: [1]..... a car?
_{you/fix}

WALT: No, [2]..... . But [3]..... my brother's motorcycle.
_{I/fix}

JOE: A motorcycle isn't a car, you know. [4]..... car mechanics?
_{you/study}

WALT: No, [5]..... . But, I'm sure I can fix it.

JOE: Why don't you take it to a mechanic?

WALT: [6]..... my mechanic's bill.
_{you/not see}

JOE: It can't be as expensive as buying a new car. [7]..... at new
_{you/look}
car prices?

WALT: Yes [8]..... . Hmm. Maybe, [9]..... enough experience with cars.
_{I/not had}

5 Talk in Pairs

1. Make up five *have you
ever...* questions. Go around
and ask at least five
classmates your questions.

2. Report to the class.

a.

b.

c.

d.

RECEPTION

e.

1. The pictures illustrate what Danny did yesterday. Write a paragraph about his activities. Include the words: *first, then, next, after that, finally.*

2. 🔲 Listen to different people talk about a problem. Write a possible comment for each one. Use: *might (not), can(not), will (not)* or *should (not).*

3. Fill in the blanks with the correct form of the following verbs.

look up see turn walk be talk go

notice hit have get crash

I ¹..... home from school yesterday when I ²..... a terrible experience. Michelle and I ³..... about our next basketball practice, so we (not) ⁴..... a green car coming really fast down our side of the street. When we ⁵..... , we ⁶..... the green car and we also ⁷..... a big yellow truck. The big yellow truck ⁸..... the corner just as the green car ⁹..... through the intersection. The car ¹⁰..... quickly to avoid the truck, and almost ¹¹..... us. Instead, it ¹²..... into Milton's Bakery. You should have seen the mess. There ¹³..... doughnuts and cookies and all kinds of bread all over the place. Fortunately, nobody ¹⁴..... hurt, but Michelle and I ¹⁵..... the fright of our lives.

4. Write the correct tag question.

a. She's coming tomorrow, ... ?

b. They didn't go downtown, ... ?

c. Mike was really frustrated yesterday, ... ?

d. The Smiths are very nice people, ... ?

e. Jessie can't come tomorrow, ... ?

5. Complete the following sentences with *(not) too* or *(not) enough* and the adjective.

a. You're only 14 years old. You're ..... to drive.
   _{old}

b. Sally is 22 years old. I think she's ..... to
   _{old}
   know better.

c. Is it ..... in here? I can close the window if
   _{cold}
   you like.

d. I'll finish this job tonight. I'm ..... yet.
   _{tired}

e. Do you think my essay is ..... ? Our teacher
   _{long}
   says it has to have at least 250 words.

6. Write the doctor's questions about your friend, who is unconscious.

a. DOCTOR: ..... ?

   YOU: I don't think so. At least, I've
         never seen it happen before.

b. DOCTOR: ..... ?

   YOU: Yes, he was in the hospital last year
         when he broke his finger.

c. DOCTOR: ..... ?

   YOU: Yes, his parents live on Fairbanks
         Drive.

d. DOCTOR: ..... ?

   YOU: Yes, I've called several times, but no
         one answers the phone.

7. Find the errors and correct them.

a. We should to do that work right now.

b. John didn't really think that, didn't he?

c. Bob says that the glue is enough dry now.

d. We were listen to music when it happened.

e. Let's finish quickly. It might can rain.

f. Have ever you heard about the Loch Ness
   monster?

g. The second concert was as better as the
   first one.

8. Look at the illustrations and complete the following sentences.

a. Sally is just ..... her brother.

b. The hotel is ..... building in this city.

c. Pineapple is ..... fruit in this market.

d. Mrs. Clyde is not ..... Mr. Clyde.

Before You Read

What do you know about sharks? Talk to your partner.
Share your ideas with the class.

Recently, *Fascinating People* **magazine talked to Ron and Valerie Taylor about their experiences with underwater photography. Here's what they told us.**

SHARKS!

FP MAGAZINE: Where are you two from, and what do you do?

VALERIE: We're from Australia and we're underwater photographers. We film sharks and other sea animals for movies and TV programs.

FP MAGAZINE: What are the most famous movies that you've worked on?

VALERIE: *Blue Water, White Death* and *Jaws.*

FP MAGAZINE: How did you get started in this business?

RON: Well, both Valerie and I started diving in the ocean near Sydney when we were teenagers. Besides, I liked to take pictures, so one day I made

a waterproof case for a movie camera so I could film under the water. I filmed a lot of sharks. Then I started selling my film for movies, TV and newsreels. After Valerie and I met, she helped me by taking photographs and by getting sharks, sea turtles, moray eels and manta rays to swim in front of my camera so I could film them.

FP MAGAZINE: That sounds pretty dangerous to me! Have you had any frightening experiences?

VALERIE: We sure have. While I was diving one day, I felt something swimming close to me. When I turned my head, I saw a huge tiger shark about 15 feet long. You can imagine how terrified I was!

FP MAGAZINE: What did you do?

VALERIE: Before I could do anything, the shark just looked at me and swam away.

1 Reading

1. Read the interview and then answer the questions that follow.

2. Answer TRUE or FALSE.
a. Ron and Valerie film only sharks.
b. Ron usually takes movies and Valerie usually takes pictures.
c. Ron and Valerie started diving when they were children.
d. The tiger shark didn't do anything to Ron.

3. Read the interview again and complete the questions the interviewer asks.
a. Where ..... ?   d. How ..... ?
b. What ..... ?   e. Have ..... ?
c. What are ..... ?   f. What ..... ?

4. Imagine that you are the interviewer. What other questions might you ask Ron and Valerie?

2 Vocabulary Building DICT

1. Synonyms are words that mean the same. Find synonyms of the following words in the article.

a. adolescents
b. a film
c. began

d. scary
e. gigantic
f. near

2. Find the word *waterproof* in the dictionary. Now write definitions for the following words:

soundproof   shockproof   bombproof

3 Listening

Listen to the rest of the interview with Ron and Valerie. Complete the questions the interviewer asks them.

a. Can ..... ?
b. Have ..... hurt?
c. What ..... toward sharks?

4 Talk in Pairs

Imagine that you are one of these people. Your partner will ask you questions about your job. Make up the answers.

a.
b.
c.
d.

5 Writing

1. Study the chart below

Time clauses starting with:

when	**When** we **saw** him, he **was trying** to climb into the boat. **When** he saw us, he **waved** his arms.
after	**After** we **rescued** him, we **took** him to the hospital.
before	**Before** I **learned** to swim, I **was** terrified of the water.
while	**While** he **was swimming**, it **started** to rain.

2. Read the article again. Find an example of each of the time clauses above.

3. A sentence with a time clause can be written in two ways. Look at the following examples.

When he saw us, he waved his arms.
He waved his arms when he saw us.

Rewrite the sentences with time clauses from the article in the other possible way.

4. Think of a time when you were in a frightening or dangerous situation. Write a composition describing the event. Follow this outline:

Paragraph 1:   Where were you?
Who was with you?
How old were you?
What time of year was it?
What was the weather like?
Paragraph 2:   What happened?
Paragraph 3:   What was the result?

At the Start

1. Do any children you know have Barbie dolls? Do you think Barbie dolls are good or bad for young girls? Read the article and find out how popular Barbie dolls are.

Who has had 5 million wedding dresses and never been married? Why Barbie, of course! And although she's never been married, she is very faithful. She has dated her boyfriend, Ken, for over thirty years. She's also had a remarkable number of careers. She has been a nurse, a police officer, a flight attendant, a fashion editor, a veterinarian, a television executive, a movie star and a heart surgeon. She has even won an Olympic gold medal and traveled in space.

Barbie's maker, Mattel, buys more cloth than anyone else in the world. They need it to make the more than 20 million new outfits Barbie owners buy each year. (They're also big on shoes. They've made more than one billion pairs for her.)

She may only be 11½ inches tall, but Barbie is big. Forget Nintendo and Sega — Barbie is the world's most popular toy. Since she was created in 1959, people have bought more than 600,000,000 Barbies. If you put them end to end, they would circle the earth three and a half times!

2. Write the numbers in words and the words in numbers.

a. 600,000,000   c. 20 million
b. one billion   d. 11½

1 Dictionary Work

1. Find the occupations named in the article. Put them into a table like the one below.

Nouns	Compound Nouns
nurse	police officer

2. Which compound nouns are in the dictionary?

3. Write definitions for the ones that aren't.

> ! I have not gone. = I haven't gone.
> • She has gone. = She's gone.
> I have finished. = I've finished.

2 Spotlight

1. Study the structures below.

I	haven't been	to New York *for six months.*
You	have owned	three cars *since you were 18.*
He	has been	her boyfriend *for 30 years.*
She	hasn't won	a gold medal *for a long time.*
We	haven't had	an exam *since March.*
They	have bought	millions of Barbies *since 1959.*

2. Find all the examples of present perfect tense in the article. Which ones use *for* or *since*?

3. What tense is used in each of these sentences?
a. She went to New York three days ago.
   (at a specific time)
b. She has gone to New York three times since January.
   (at unspecified times with the chance she will again)
c. He didn't visit us when he was in the U.S.
   (there is no more chance that he will)
d. He hasn't visited us for five years.
   (there is still a chance that he will)
e. He called her every day for two years.
   (he doesn't anymore)

4. Look at the sentences in 3 again and complete the rules using *for, since* and *ago*.
a. Use ..... before a period of time completely in the past, with the simple past.
b. Use ..... before a specific time in the past, with the present perfect.
c. Use ..... after a period of time starting from now into the past, with the simple past.
d. Use ..... before a period of time starting in the past and continuing to the present, with present perfect.

3 Practice

Use the simple past or present perfect.

My Aunt Sylvia ¹..... a very exciting life. She and Uncle Paul ²..... _{have}   _{be}
married for forty years. Before he ³..... he and Aunt Sylvia ⁴..... _{die}   _{take}
wonderful vacations to exotic places such as Kenya and New Guinea. Since his death, Aunt Sylvia ⁵..... traveling. She ⁶..... _{not stop}   _{visit}
India and ⁷..... an elephant. She ⁸..... big game hunting in Africa, _{ride}   _{go}
with a camera of course! Last year, at the age of 76, she ⁹..... a _{climb}
mountain in Nepal! I really admire Aunt Sylvia. I guess she ¹⁰..... _{do}
about everything that there is to do.

4 Listening

Carl makes model railroads. Read the questions and then listen to the interview for the answers.
a. How long has he been interested in trains?
b. How long has he had a model railroad?
c. How long ago did he get sick?
d. How long was he unable to work?
e. When did he quit his job?
f. How many trains has he made since 1986?

5 Talk in Pairs

1. Tell your partner about things you like to do but haven't done for a long time. Explain why you haven't done them. Use *for, since* and *ago*.

2. Tell the class about what your partner hasn't done and why.

At the Start

1. Do you ever get headaches? What do you do? Read the following article for some great tips.

How to Avoid a Headache

We can't help getting headaches sometimes. But there are some ways to avoid getting them too often.

1 Try to eat and sleep on a regular schedule. Missing meals or going to bed later than usual can cause a headache.

2 Stop drinking coffee. If you need to drink coffee, don't drink more than two cups a day, or drink decaffeinated coffee. Some research says that caffeine can cause headaches.

3 Avoid staying in smoke-filled rooms. The smoke can cause a headache.

4 Exercise regularly. Exercise helps reduce stress which can cause headaches.

5 Headaches can also be caused by foods that we all enjoy eating. Some common foods that can cause headaches are: chocolate, pickles, cheese, cream, yogurt.

6 If you get frequent headaches, consider keeping a headache journal. Write down when you get headaches. This will help you and your doctor find their cause.

2. According to the article, which of these can cause headaches?

> caffeine   exercise   missing meals   smoke
> coffee   research   stress   a headache journal

1 Dictionary Work   DICT

1. Look up the pronunciation of these words in the dictionary:
journal   headache   frequent   cause   schedule

Check your pronunciation with your partner.

2. Which word is pronounced differently in British English? How is it pronounced?

3. Which of these verbs can be followed by either *verb + -ing* (gerund) or *to + verb* (infinitive)?
try   avoid   stop   enjoy   like

2 Spotlight

1. Study the structures below.

	avoid can't help keep on regret consider	
I		**drinking** coffee in the morning.

	want need try agree decide remember forget	
I		**to drink** coffee in the morning.

> **!** Some verbs can take gerunds or **infinitives**. For example: *I hate swimming./ I hate to swim. I like studying./ I like to study.*

2. Look at the article. Find as many examples of each structure as you can.

3 Listening

1. 🔲 Listen for the questions on this survey and complete them.
a. What do you ..... ?
b. What household chore do you ..... ?
c. Is there anything that you often ..... ?
d. What do you ..... ?
e. Is there anything that you ..... to improve your life?
f. What do you ..... ?

2. 🔲 Listen again and match these answers to the correct questions.
1. Answering your questions.
2. Exercise.
3. Washing the dishes.
4. Go back to school.
5. Go to the post office.
6. Housework.

4 Practice

1. Make sentences from the questions and answers in 3.
Example:
She hates washing the dishes.

2. Look at the questions in 3. Answer them for yourself and make sentences.

3. Complete these questions for a survey.

a.	What do you avoid ..... ?
b.	What do you hate ..... ?
c.	What do you like ..... ?
d.	What do you mind ..... ?
e.	What do you need ..... ?
f.	What do you remember ..... ?
g.	What do you try ..... ?
h.	What do you want ..... ?

5 Talk in Pairs

1. Ask several classmates the questions you wrote in 4. Write down their answers.

2. Report the most interesting answers to your class.

Before You Read

1. Look quickly through the article and answer these questions.

a. This article probably appeared in (a newspaper/ a magazine).

b. A hum is (a picture/ a sound).

c. Taos is (a place/a machine).

2. Look at the headline. What does the word *still* mean?

1 Reading

1. Read the article and check your answers.

2. Answer these questions.

a. How does the article define the Taos hum?

b. How do most people who hear the noise describe it?

c. Paragraph five suggests three possible causes of the hum. What are they?

3. Answer TRUE or FALSE.

a. Everybody in the Taos area can hear the hum.

b. People in other countries cannot hear the hum.

c. The hum is louder inside the house than outside.

d. The hum is annoying, but it does not cause any physical problems.

The Taos Hum Is Still A Mystery

Associated Press, Santa Fe, New Mexico.

The Taos hum, a low-frequency sound that only some people can hear, remains a mystery. Investigators, both scientists and engineers, cannot find the source of this strange and annoying noise, and the sensitive instruments they have used show nothing.

People have complained about the hum in the Taos area since 1991. However, even before that time, in 1989, there were similar complaints about an irritating hum in Albuquerque. When news of the Taos hum was published, people in other states, such as Michigan, Vermont, Massachusetts, New York and Maryland also reported hearing the hum. Even people in other countries, such as Taiwan, say they have heard the same sound.

Most people who hear the noise say that it begins abruptly, never stops, prevents them from sleeping, and is stronger inside the house than outside. Some describe the noise like a motor running softly in the distance. Other people say the noise is responsible for their headaches, nosebleeds and dizziness.

Scientists have not been able to discover the cause of the noise by investigating it directly, so they are now going to study the people who can hear it. They are trying to understand why some people can hear it while others cannot, even though they live in the same area.

Some scientists feel that electromagnetic fields along the ground may be connected to the noise, but there is no proof. Other scientists are considering the possibility that some people are extremely sensitive to the electromagnetic noise from electric appliances, microwave ovens and cordless phones. Another possible explanation is that in some people, the ear itself produces sounds.

2 Vocabulary Building DICT

1. Look at the words in the box.

Verb	Adjective
annoy	annoying
irritate	irritating

2. Form adjectives from these verbs.
a. gurgle   c. terrify   e. pound
b. disgust   d. soothe

Which ones do you think are pleasant or unpleasant? If you do not know the meaning of the verbs, check in the dictionary.

3. Complete the following sentences with one of the adjectives above.
a. Listening to classical music can be very ..... .
b. Some children find sleeping in the dark ..... .
c. The ..... waves kept him awake.
d. Babies often make little ..... noises.
e. What a ..... noise. It makes me want to stop eating.

3 Listening

🔊 Listen to the sounds on the tape and match them to the pictures. Describe them with one or more of the adjectives above.

4 Talk in Pairs or Groups

1. Think of a recent experience. Try to remember where you were, who was with you, and exactly what happened. Tell your story to a group of your classmates.

2. Choose the most interesting story in the group. Then choose one person from the group to tell that story to the whole class.

5 Writing

1. Look at the sentences in the box.

The concert was terrible, **so** I went home.
The theater was small, **and** it was crowded.
It was late, **but** the concert still didn't start.

2. In the reading, find an example of two sentences joined by *and*, *but* or *so*.

3. Look at the sentences in the box and complete the rules.
a. To join two related ideas use ..... .
b. To join a cause and an effect, use ..... .
c. To join two contradicting ideas, use ..... .
d. When we connect two ideas with *and*, *but* or *so*, we usually put a ..... before *and*, *but* or *so*.

4. Connect the following sentences with *and*, *but* or *so*.
a. The soft music was very soothing. It didn't make her feel better.
b. He made a lot of noise drinking his coffee. I got up and left.
c. The boys put on some heavy metal music. They listened to it for hours.

5. 🔊 Listen to someone describing an experience. Do the dictation.

6. Write about your recent experience.
Paragraph 1: Write about where you were, and who was with you.
Paragraph 2: Write about what happened, and why it was pleasant or unpleasant.

At the Start

1. Look at the picture of the child. How does she feel?

2. Now read the poster and answer the questions.
a. What are the four things that the poster says that all children need?
b. What are many children not getting?

Have you hugged your child yet today?

Millions of busy parents think that they're already doing a good job because their children have food, clothes and a place to live. Unfortunately, they've forgotten another necessity: love. So even if you've already hugged your child today, do it again. Nobody ever gets too many hugs.

1 Dictionary Work `DICT`

1. Look up the pronunciation of these words. In which two is *un-* pronounced differently?
unnatural   united   unlucky
uniform   uncommon

2. Find five other words that begin with *un-*. What are their opposites?

2 Spotlight

1. Study the structures below.

Have you **finished** your work **yet**?
– Yes, I've **already finished**.
– No, I **haven't**.

Have they **already finished** working?
– Yes, they **have**.
– No, they **haven't** finished **yet**.

Has he **washed** the dishes **yet**?
– Yes, he's **already washed** the dishes.
– No, he **hasn't washed** them **yet**.

2. Look at the structures and put *already* and *yet* in the correct categories.

questions	
negative statements	
positive statements	

3 Listening

1. **Listen to the conversation and answer the questions.**
a. Who are the speakers?
b. Which one has a problem?
c. What's his problem?

2. **Listen again and check the things that Mike has done.**
a. gone to speak to the administration
b. asked about other scholarships
c. got a part-time job
d. started looking for a job
e. asked about studying part-time
f. worked in a library

4 Practice

1. Make sentences about what Mike has *already* done and what he hasn't done *yet*.

2. Look at the list below and say what you've *already* done and what you haven't done *yet*.
a. finished high school
b. learned to swim
c. gotten married
d. had a baby
e. learned to drive a car
f. started working
g. lived on your own
h. retired

5 Role Play

Student A: You and Student B are roommates. You think your roommate doesn't do enough around the house. Today he or she hasn't:
washed the dishes.
taken out the garbage.
vacuumed the floor.

Student B: You think that you do more than your roommate does. This week you have:
cooked dinner three times.
done the laundry.
vacuumed the floor.

Have a conversation starting like this:
A: Betty, we have to talk. I don't think you're doing your share of the chores. You haven't washed the dishes yet and it's 10 p.m.
B: I do a lot around here. I've already vacuumed the floor...

6 Pronunciation

 The pronunciation of some pronouns often changes in normal speech. Listen to these examples.
a. Has he come home yet?
b. I already gave him the address.
c. We told her to be here at eight.
d. She asked them if they wanted to come.

Listen again and repeat the sentences.

At the Start

1. What do you think makes a person interesting?

2. Take this personality quiz and find out if you are interesting or boring.

Are you Boring?

3. Turn to page 69 for your score.

1 Dictionary Work DICT

1. Look up the *-ed* and *-ing* adjective forms of these verbs.
confuse   terrify   amaze   surprise

2. Complete these rules about the spelling of *-ed* and *-ing* adjectives.
a. When the verb ends in *y* change the ..... to ..... then add ....
b. When the verb ends in *e* just add ..... instead of *-ed*.
c. When the verb ends in *e* drop the ..... before you add ..... .

1. Your friends are excited about going to a movie by a famous French director. (You've heard that it's very strange.) Your friends invite you to go with them, so you say:
a. "Sorry. I don't like foreign movies."
b. "Why don't you go and tell me what it's like?"
c. "Sounds interesting. Let's go."

2. You're at a new restaurant with some friends. It's your turn to order, so you:
a. order something that you have never eaten before.
b. order what your best friend ordered.
c. order a hamburger.

3. You have a free Saturday:
a. you are bored, so you watch TV.
b. you are tired, so you take a long nap.
c. you go to the art museum to see a new exhibit.

4. You are head of a group to earn money for an organization. You decide to:
a. think of some exciting new ways to raise money.
b. send out information to all the members.
c. sell candy, since that worked before.

5. A new classmate is interested in you. He/She seems nice but very different from your friends, so you:
a. stay away. He/she is not your type.
b. decide to get to know him/her better. He/she might be interesting.
c. ask your friends what they think.

2 Spotlight

1. Study the structures below.

I'm **bored**.
You're **excited**.
They're **terrified**.

This is a **boring** class.
What an **exciting** day!
The movie is **terrifying**.

2. Look at the quiz again. Find a pair of *-ed* and *-ing* adjectives.

3. Now match a pair of adjectives with these phrases.
Joe, the football fan, goes to the World Cup.
The World Cup.

3 Listening

1. 🖭 Listen to the conversation and make sentences about the opinions of the man and the woman.

The man thinks that	hang-gliding bowling aerobics	is	interesting. boring. exhausting. exciting. terrifying. relaxing.
The woman thinks that			

2. 🖭 Listen again and answer these questions.
a. Who feels **frightened?** Why?
b. Who feels **confused?** Why?

4 Practice

1. Complete the sentences with the correct adjective form of one of the verbs.

> **!** *-ed* adjectives usually take a preposition.

bore (by)   disappoint (in)   excite (about)
exhaust (from)   fascinate (by)   frighten (of)
terrify (of)   tire (from)   interest (in)

a. I thought it was a ..... lecture. *I fell asleep.*
b. She's ..... her daughter. *She gets C's and D's.*
c. My son is ..... flying. *He doesn't like it.*
d. They're ..... their vacation. *They can't wait.*
e. I collect stamps because I think they're ..... .
f. They have a big ..... dog. *He scares me.*
g. Driving can be ..... . *It's easy to fall asleep.*

2. Change the sentences in 1 to use the other form of the adjective.
Example:
a. *I was bored by the lecture.*

5 Talk in Pairs

Look at the pictures of these people. How do you feel about each activity? How do you think the people feel?

Before You Read

1. How many brothers and sisters does an only child have?

2. Look at the title of the article. Does it suggest that it's good or bad to be an only child?

1 Reading

1. Read the article and see if you were right.

2. Complete the chart. What are the advantages and disadvantages of being an only child?

Being an only child	
advantages	disadvantages

3. Answer TRUE or FALSE.
a. It is definitely better to be an only child.
b. Only children generally make decisions very quickly.
c. Only children are always maladjusted and spoiled.
d. Children from larger families usually feel great pressure to succeed.

ONLY BUT NOT LONELY

My family.

For many years, research has suggested that being an only child causes many problems. According to recent studies, however, it seems that only children have no more difficulties than other children – just different ones.

In fact, in some ways, only children are better off. Karen Lipman, a family therapist in New York, says that in the past, people thought that only children were always isolated and without friends. Ms. Lipman, however, insists that often children from large families feel as isolated as only children. Furthermore, she claims that only children form closer and longer relationships with cousins or friends.

James Rourke, a psychologist from Denver, Colorado, says that although people think that only children are maladjusted and spoiled, his research shows that only children usually show great initiative, have high levels of self-esteem and good mental health. They are generally more reliable, more organized, more attentive and more interested in their studies than other children. They think carefully before making any decisions.

Nevertheless, being an only child is not the answer to all of life's problems, either. Only children receive a great deal of attention from their parents and, as a result, sometimes feel too much pressure to succeed. Because they feel very special at home, they sometimes expect the rest of the world to treat them as special, too. Some become too demanding. Others do not have the opportunity to be children because they are always treated as adults.

Perhaps it does not matter so much if a child is an only child or a member of a larger family. Perhaps what is more important is for every child to be treated with love and respect.

2 Vocabulary Building `DICT`

1. Look at the adjectives in the box. Look in the article and find their opposites.

unreliable	disorganized
uninterested	inattentive
undemanding	unspoiled

2. *un-* is a prefix which gives the original word an opposite meaning. Look at the list above. What are two other prefixes that do the same thing?

3. Look at the following examples. Then complete the sentences.
He is a careful child. He thinks carefully.
a. Careful refers to the noun ....., so it is an adjective.
b. Carefully refers to the verb ....., so it is an adverb.
c. Most adjectives can be made into adverbs by adding ..... .

4. Complete the following sentences with the correct adjective or adverb, or its opposite.

a. That child always listens to the teacher very ..... .
_{attentive}

b. She is the most ..... person
_{organized}
I know. She is always losing things.

c. She's a very creative child. She likes to do things ..... .
_{different}

d. A demanding child is ..... .
_{pleasant}

3 Listening

Listen to the conversation. Use the adjectives in the box in 2 or their opposites to describe Carol and Scott.

4 Talk in Pairs or Groups

Ask these questions.
a. What is your position in your family? Are you the oldest, youngest, in the middle or the only child?
b. How does your position in the family affect you?
c. Do you have cousins? friends? Describe your relationships with them.

5 Writing

Write a composition about the advantages and disadvantages of being the oldest, youngest or middle child in a family. Use the following pattern.
Paragraph 1: Explain what the advantages are.
Paragraph 2: Explain what the disadvantages are.
Paragraph 3: Explain how you feel about the advantages and disadvantages.

Review 2: Units 8–14

1. Connect each set of sentences. Use *when, before, after* or *while.*

a. We heard the news. We went to the hospital immediately.

b. It was raining. We stayed inside.

c. You should do some warm-up activities. You play basketball.

d. I took a shower. I got dressed.

2. Complete the following sentences with the right form of the adjective.

a. Everyone was really ..... about going on the camping trip. _{excite}

b. This problem is so ...... I can't solve it. _{confuse}

c. The ..... part of the experience was coming back down. _{frighten}

d. The children were ..... when they came home from the expedition. _{exhaust}

e. All the students were ..... with their grades. _{disappoint}

3. Combine each pair of sentences. Use *and, so* or *but.*

a. These math questions are really difficult. I think I can do them.

b. About thirty of us went to have lunch together. The restaurant was pretty crowded.

c. That family has lived in this city for generations. Most people know them.

d. They worked on the project for a couple of hours. Then they went for a walk.

e. I've spoken to our new neighbor a few times. I still don't know his name.

4. Look at the pictures. Write sentences about what Harry has and has not done. Use *yet* or *already* in each of your sentences.

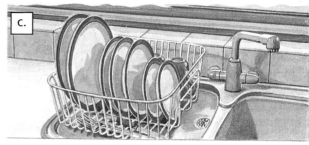

5. Complete the following sentences.

a. Last night, I decided ..... .

b. My friend has really tried ..... .

c. What do you think? We were considering ..... .

d. Sometimes children can't help ..... .

e. Does everyone agree ..... ?

6. Complete the following article by putting the verbs in the correct tense (present, past, past continuous, or present perfect).

Jeanie Greene ¹..... her
_{have}
own TV show since
1990. At first, the show
²..... of five-minute news
_{consist}
segments. However, it
³..... so popular that
_{become}
Jeanie Greene ⁴..... a
_{develop}
new show called

Heartbeat Alaska. What is so special about the show and about Jeanie Greene? Jeanie Greene is an Inupiat Eskimo. She ⁵..... born in a fishing
_{be}
town called Sitka, in southeast Alaska, in 1952. As a child, she ⁶..... ballet and gymnastics
_{take}
lessons, and in college, she ⁷..... anthropology
_{study}
and theater.

While she ⁸..... her degree, she ⁹..... in more than
_{get}   _{act}
50 plays. She ¹⁰..... her own Anchorage theater
_{manage}
company since 1986. Now her show, Heartbeat Alaska, ¹¹..... popular, not only in Alaska, but
_{become}
also throughout the U.S. In her shows, she ¹².....
_{discuss}
serious problems such as teenage suicide, but her main goal ¹³..... always to defend her
_{be}
people's culture.

7. Complete the sentences with one of the following words or with its opposite.

annoying   spoiled   soothing   attentive
reliable

a. I suppose this is a terrible thing to say, but I really don't like that child. She is too ..... .

b. We can't ask Tim to take charge of anything. He is completely ..... .

c. Please close the window. I'm trying to work, and the noise from outside is very ..... .

d. That doctor has a very ..... voice. He can always make his patients relax.

e. As soon as spring comes, the children become so ..... at school. Everything distracts them.

8. 🔲 Listen to the tape, look at the picture and do the dictation.

9. Write three questions that you would like to ask Mr. Cox.

15

At the Start

1. Who lives in a haunted house? Do you believe in ghosts? Have you ever seen a ghost? Tell your classmates and your teacher.

2. Read this article about one woman's experience with a ghost.

3. Now answer the questions.
a. How old is the woman's house?
b. How long ago did Dora die there?
c. Is the writer afraid of Dora?

1 Dictionary Work

1. What is the pronunciation of the word *psychic?*

2. Look at other words that begin with *psych-*. What do you think this prefix means?

3. Match these common prefixes with their meaning.
a. re-   1. after
b. pre-   2. again
c. post-   3. before

Find two words that begin with each prefix.

4. Make sentences with three of the words you found.

THE HAUNTED HOUSE

We bought our house about 10 years ago. It's very old. It was built in 1781. Soon after we moved in unusual things began happening. First we started losing things and finding them again in strange places. One day I was cooking in the kitchen and I smelled smoke. Nothing was burning on the stove. I looked outside. There was no fire there either. Once when my parents were visiting, they heard footsteps in the hall. Later, they saw a strange woman in the bedroom upstairs. A repairman found a back door wide open. He knew that the door was never used because the key was lost many years earlier. "I ran as fast as I could," he said.

That's when I called in a psychic, a person who tries to contact ghosts. The psychic told us these things. "The woman's name is Dora," he said. "She's about 60 years old. She lived in this house and died here in a fire in 1812. She likes to cook and spends a lot of time in the kitchen. You probably hear footsteps because she wears a pair of heavy boots. She doesn't know that she is dead. She thinks that she has a right to be here."

We have lived with Dora for years now and we've gotten used to her. She hasn't hurt anyone. Although I've never seen her, I often talk to her while I'm working in the kitchen.

2 Spotlight

1. Review these tenses. Match the sentences to the tense.

simple past
actions in the past one after another

past continuous/simple past
one action interrupts another action

present perfect
action that starts in the past and continues into the future

a. We've **lived** with Dora for many years.
b. They **heard** footsteps in the hall and later they **saw** a strange woman.
c. I **was cooking** when I **smelled** smoke.

2. Look at the article. Find two more examples of each tense.

3 Listening DICT

1. Look up these words in the dictionary. Are they nouns or verbs?

a. hook   c. bet   e. crawl
b. flashlight d. smash   f. swear

2. 📼 Listen to the story and complete these sentences with the words above.

a. They ..... out the window.
b. They made a ..... with their friends.
c. He had a ..... instead of a hand.
d. My grandmother ..... that it's true.
e. She ..... the window with the ..... .

3. 📼 Listen again and say TRUE or FALSE. Correct the false sentences.

a. The speaker's grandmother has always believed in ghosts.
b. Many people believed that the house was haunted.
c. The speaker's grandmother went to the house alone.
d. The two girls saw a ghost.
e. The speaker's grandmother won the bet.

4 Practice

Complete these sentences. Remember to put the verbs into the present, past, past continuous or present perfect tense.

My family ¹..... in the United States since we ²..... from Brazil in 1980. When I was 10, I ³..... to Brazil with my mother and sister. It ⁴..... my mother's first trip since my grandfather's death. We ⁵..... in my aunt's house. One night while I ⁶..... I ⁷..... my mother call me. "Don't scream," she said. "Just ⁸..... at the ceiling and ⁹..... me what you see." I ¹⁰..... and of course, I ¹¹..... . On the ceiling there ¹²..... a shadow of an old man. He ¹³..... a straw hat and ¹⁴..... a rifle. That night we ¹⁵..... all the furniture out of the room to see if it ¹⁶..... a shadow. While we ¹⁷..... the furniture, we ¹⁸..... someone knocking on the window but there ¹⁹..... no one there. I ²⁰..... stay in that house anymore. My mother, my sister and I ²¹..... in the morning and we ²²..... since that day.

(verb cues: 1 live, 2 come, 3 go back, 4 be, 5 stay, 6 sleep, 7 hear, 8 look up, 9 tell, 10 look up, 11 scream, 12 be, 13 wear, 14 carry, 15 move, 16 be, 17 move, 18 hear, 19 be, 20 can not, 21 leave, 22 not go back)

5 Talk in Pairs

Tell your partner a ghost story.

6 Writing

Write your ghost story.

16

FOUR STRONG WINDS

Four strong winds that blow lonely, seven seas that run high,
All those things that don't change, come what may,
But our good times have all gone, and I'm bound for movin' on,
I'll look for you if I'm ever back this way.

I think I'll go back to Alberta, the weather's good there in the fall,
I got some friends that I can go to workin' for,
Still, I hope you'll change your mind, if I ask you one more time,
But we've been through that a hundred times or more.

If I get there before the snow flies, and if things are lookin' good,
You can meet me if I send you down the fare,
But by then it will be winter, nothin' much for you to do,
And those winds can sure blow cold way out there.

At the Start

1. 📼 Listen to the song and look at the picture. Where is it?

2. Now complete these sentences with one of the words in parentheses.
a. The tone of the song is (happy/sad).
b. The singer is (leaving/ meeting) someone.
c. The singer is singing to his (mother/girlfriend).
d. The season is probably (mid-winter/late summer).

1 Dictionary Work DICT

1. Look up these words and phrases in the dictionary.
bound for   fare
change your mind

2. Which phrase is a common idiom? Use it in a sentence.

2 Spotlight

1. Study this structure.

If I come back, I'll call you.
I'll call you **if** I come back.

If the weather is good, you **can** visit me.
You **can** visit me **if** the weather is good.

If he has time, he's **going to** stop at the store.
He's **going to** stop at the store **if** he has time.

2. Sentences with *if* have two parts or clauses. When do you use a comma?

3. Which part of the sentence refers to the future, but uses the present tense? Which part uses a future form (*will* or *going to*) or a modal (*can, might, should*)?

4. Find examples of the structure in the song.

3 Listening

1. 🖾 Listen to this conversation and decide what the relationship between the two people is.

2. 🖾 Listen again and complete these conditional sentences.
a. Karen can leave early if ..... .
b. If Karen doesn't type the agenda, ...
c. Karen should take a message if ..... .
d. Marcy can answer the phone if ..... .
e. If Marcy isn't there ..... .

3. 🖾 Listen again for the request that Ms. Rogers makes.

4 Practice

1. Complete these conditional sentences by yourself. Then share your answers with the class.
a. If I study hard, ...
b. My best friend will be happy if ..... .
c. If you give children everything they want, ...
d. You can't get a good job if ..... .
e. If students cheat on exams, ...
f. There will be trouble in my country if ..... .
g. I won't need money if ..... .

2. Write four more clauses, two starting with *if* and two ending with *if*. Read your clauses to your partner and let him or her complete them.

5 Talk in Pairs

1. Look up the word *superstition* in the dictionary. Do you believe these common superstitions?

You will have bad luck if you walk under ladder.

If your nose itches, you will have a visitor.

You will have good luck if you find a four-leaf clover.

If you break a mirror, you will have seven years of bad luck.

2. Tell your partner some superstitions from your country.

17

FIRE!

At the Start

1. Have you ever seen a big fire? What was it like?

2. Read the article. Then answer TRUE or FALSE.
a. You cannot put out an oil fire with water.
b. Covering the well is not very dangerous.
c. People worked night and day to put out the fires in Kuwait.

Oil fires with temperatures of 3,000°F blaze all around. They roar and shoot flames as high as 400 feet. The heat is so strong that it turns sand into glass. There is so much smoke that day becomes night.

Is this a scene from a new movie? No, it is a normal day at work for fire fighters who put out oil well fires. Listen as Tom Bradden talks about his dangerous job.

"There are three main ways to put out an oil well fire. You can use water. You can use dynamite to blow up the well. You can cut off the oxygen to the fire.

"After the fire is out, you have to cap or cover the well. That's the most dangerous job because everything is covered with oil and the well could burst into flames in a second. Even after the fire is out, oil keeps on coming out. So then we have to cut off the flow of the oil.

"The most difficult fires I have ever worked on were in Kuwait. There were 600 fires and the work went on 24 hours a day. It was particularly difficult because we were in the desert. Sometimes we almost ran out of water. It was hard but we never gave up. Finally, after eight months, all the fires were out. However, the work was not finished. Even today, years after the fires, the people of Kuwait are still cleaning up."

1 Dictionary Work DICT

1. Look up the pronunciation of these words in the dictionary:

roar scene dangerous particularly special temperature

Check your pronunciation with your partner.

2. Look up these verbs in the dictionary. Which ones can have objects? (transitive [T]) Which ones cannot have objects? (intransitive [I])

run out of give up clean up cut off burst into put out
blow up come out turn into

2 Spotlight

1. Study the structures below.

Many verbs in English are formed from a verb + one or two prepositions.

Some multi-word verbs are separable.

> We **put out** the fire.   We **put** the fire **out**.
> We **put** it **out**.

When the object is a pronoun, separable verbs must be separated

> We **gave up** the fight.   We **gave** it **up**.

Some two-word verbs and all three-word verbs are inseparable.

> The car **burst into** flames.
> We almost **ran out of** water.
> I **broke up with** her last week.

2. Can you find the multi-word verbs in the article? Look at the table on page 71. Which verbs are separable and which are inseparable?

3 Listening

🔲 Listen to the conversation. Check the multi-word verbs you hear from the list below.

call off	break up with	call up	catch on
get off	get on	get to	hand in
keep on	look forward to	look up	put off
sign up	throw out	turn out	wake up
hold up	run out of	work out	fill out

4 Practice

🔲 Listen again and answer the questions about the listening. Use the multi-word verbs from the list above.

a. What didn't Carol do?
b. Why didn't she do it?
c. What did they do in class?
d. What's the homework?
e. Is there class tomorrow? Why or why not?

5 Talk in Pairs

Look at these pictures. Make up a story with your partner. Use at least ten multi-word verbs.

18

Before You Read DICT

1. Look up the words *lottery* and *pawnshop* in your dictionary.

2. Use each word in a sentence.

1 Reading

1. Read the following article.

The State Lottery Has a New Winner

Associated Press, Trenton, N.J.

Although the results of the New Jersey state lottery have left many people feeling disappointed, they have also left one family with hope for the future.

The day before the winners were announced, Brad and Elaine Sanders emptied their pockets and put their money on the table. It came to exactly $1.03.

When the sawmill closed down nine months before, Brad tried to find a job in the city. No jobs of any kind were available. His wife, Elaine, said the family could continue to survive on her salary as a pilot of a little crop spraying plane. Then, disaster struck again. Three weeks after Brad lost his job, Elaine's plane went out of control, and she had to make a crash landing. Fortunately, Elaine only had a broken leg. The plane, however, needed major repairs. So on that day, Brad, Elaine, and their three children, Jason, Rick and Sally, stared forlornly at the $1.03 lying on the table.

The family meeting lasted long into the night. Finally, everyone agreed that on the following day, they would take Elaine's jewelry to the pawnshop.

The next morning, the phone rang. An unknown voice asked Brad if he had read the paper that day. Brad laughed and said that he didn't have enough money to buy the paper. The voice answered that he didn't think that was quite true, because $4.2 million dollars was more than enough to buy a newspaper.

Needless to say, the Sanders did not take Elaine's jewelry to the pawnshop.

2. Put the following sentences in the order in which they happened.
a. The Sanders realized they had only $1.03.
b. Elaine's plane crashed.
c. The family had a meeting about money.
d. The sawmill closed.
e. The Sanders family won the lottery.
f. The family decided to take Elaine's jewelry to the pawnshop.

2 Vocabulary Building   DICT

1. **Match the compound nouns with their meanings.**

a. state lottery
b. crop spraying plane
c. crash landing

1. a landing with a crash
2. a lottery run by the state
3. a plane that sprays crops

2. **Read the following descriptions, and write the compound nouns.**

Example:
a store that sells groceries – grocery store

a. a box to put jewelry in
b. a book about history
c. an album to put photos in
d. a coat used in a lab

3 Listening

1. 📼 Listen to Mr. Adams talk about his experience of winning the lottery.

2. 📼 Listen again and answer TRUE or FALSE.

a. Mr. Adams won the lottery three years ago.
b. Mr. Adams is an electrician.
c. The first thing Mr. Adams bought was a car.
d. Mr. Adams' children are in college.
e. Mr. Adams is divorced.

3. **Mr. Adams thinks that his wife is happy. Do you think that Mr. Adams is happy? Why or why not?**

4 Talk in Pairs or Groups

1. **Do you like to buy or sell lottery tickets? Why or why not?**

2. **Have you ever won anything? Talk about the occasion, even if you won something very small.**

3. **Do you know anyone who is either very lucky or unlucky?**

5 Writing

1. **A topic sentence gives the main idea of an article. What is the topic sentence of the article in this unit?**

2. **Look at the following topic sentence. What is the article going to be about?**
Throughout the years, educators have developed many theories about the best way to learn a foreign language.

3. **Write a topic sentence for one of the following ideas.**

a. Your experience when you won something.
b. A story about someone else winning something.

4. **Following the topic sentence you wrote in 3, write a composition following this outline.**
Paragraph 1: Write your topic sentence. Elaborate a little by explaining if what you are going to talk about was good or bad for you, or both.
Paragraph 2: Talk about the actual experience.
Paragraph 3: Explain how you felt as a result of the experience.

19

At the Start DICT

1. Look up the word *kidnapped*. What do you think *dognapped* means?

2. Read the article and find out why the dog was stolen.

Dognapped!

Fifi, Mrs. Meredith Morgan's prize French poodle, was kidnapped from Riverside Park late yesterday afternoon.

Mrs. Morgan's maid, Grace Roberts, was taking the dog for her afternoon walk when she (the dog) was grabbed by two men.

Ms. Roberts' screams were heard by two men in the park. They chased the kidnappers, but were not able to catch them.

An immediate report was sent out to all police cars in the area. Fifteen minutes later the men and the dog were seen a few blocks from the park. They were followed by a police officer until help arrived.

The men, Thomas Patterson and William Gates, were arrested and Fifi was returned to Mrs. Morgan.

Patterson and Gates said that they took the dog because Mrs. Morgan didn't pay them for work they had done. Mrs. Morgan had no comment.

1 Dictionary Work DICT

Are these verbs transitive or intransitive or both? How are they used in the text?

arrest chase follow grab hear kidnap
see take

2 Spotlight

1. Study the past passive structure below.

	past *be* + past participle
The dog	**was kidnapped** (by two men).
	The two men kidnapped the dog.
Two men	**were arrested** (by the police).
	The police arrested the men.

2. Look at the article. Underline the past passive voice verbs. Compare with the list of transitive verbs. What can you say about the kinds of verbs that can be used in the passive?

3 Listening

1. 🖭 Listen to these two conversations about the same event. Which one uses more passive voice? Why?

2. 🖭 Read the following questions. Then listen again for the answers.
a. How did the thieves enter the house?
b. What was stolen?
c. What was broken?
d. What was turned over?
e. What was thrown on the floor?
f. What mistake did the thieves make?

46

4 Practice

1. Change the following sentences to passive voice.
a. The police officer chased the thieves.
b. Shakespeare wrote this play.
c. The doctor took her to the hospital.
d. Terrorists kidnapped the men.
e. All the neighbors saw her.
f. Paul drove the car.

2. Change the following sentences to the active voice.
a. The boy was hit by a speeding car.
b. The children were frightened by the loud noise.
c. The necklace was stolen by an employee.
d. The rumor was started by his jealous cousin.
e. The school was built by the government.

3. Use the past passive voice to describe the things that were done to this room. What was stolen?

5 Talk in Pairs

Think about when you were younger and didn't have any responsibilities. What was done for you?
Example:
My meals were cooked for me.

6 Pronunciation

1. 🔊 Listen to the pronunciation of these past passive phrases. Notice the shortened sound of *was* and the quick *-n* sound at the end.

was driven   was eaten
was stolen   was broken
was hidden   was written

2. 🔊 Now listen and repeat these sentences.
a. The stolen car was driven over a cliff.
b. Their meal was eaten in a hurry.
c. Her dog was stolen by the two men.
d. A window was broken.
e. A lot of cash was hidden in the safe.
f. The message was written on the wall.

At the Start

Sue is looking for a job. Read Sue and Karen's conversation. Then match the company names with the people Sue talked to.

KAREN: How's your job-hunting going?

SUE: OK. I talked to five people today.

KAREN: What happened? What did they say?

SUE: Well, Acme Insurance said that they couldn't hire me because I had never studied typing.

KAREN: Where else did you go?

SUE: Then I went to Bill's Canoe Shop. They said that they were sorry. They had already hired someone else.

KAREN: That's bad luck.

SUE: Then I talked to someone at Seaway Furniture store. They said that they needed someone with more experience.

KAREN: Oh dear.

SUE: After that I talked to the manager at the Midway Cafe but he said that he didn't need anyone right now, but he would call me when they had a vacancy.

KAREN: Sounds like a pretty discouraging day.

SUE: Yes, I was discouraged alright. Finally, I went to Southern Bus Company and they said I could start on Monday.

KAREN: Great!

1 Dictionary Work DICT

1. Look up the pronunciation of these words. The letters in bold in each group have different pronunciations. Work with your partner to practice the differences.

int**er**view/exp**er**ience
j**o**b/w**o**men
S**ou**thern/c**ou**ld
h**ea**rt/alr**ea**dy
Acm**e**/caf**e**

2. Look up the pronunciation of these words. Then match the sounds of the letters in bold with one of the words above.

b**u**s th**ou**ght h**ea**r s**ai**d n**ee**d

2 Spotlight

1. Study the structures below.

direct speech	reported speech
"I **don't need** anyone right now but I**'ll call** you when we have a vacancy."	She said (that) **she didn't need** anyone now but (that) she **would call** me when they had a vacancy.
"I**'m** sorry. We**'ve already hired** someone."	He said (that) he **was** sorry. They **had already hired** someone.
"I **need** someone with more experience."	He said (that) **he needed** someone with more experience.
"**You can** start next Monday."	She said (that) **I could** start next Monday.

2. Look at the example sentences and complete the table.

In reported statements		
present tense		.....
have/has		.....
can		.....
will	changes to	.....
I		.....
We		.....
You		.....

3 Listening

1. 📻 Listen to this conversation between two friends and then complete these statements.

a. Tina and Carl are talking about a ..... .
b. They both think that it sounds like a ..... job.
c. The salary is ..... .
d. The job is taking tours of ..... to ..... .
e. The tour guide must speak ..... , or ..... and ..... .
f. To apply you should ..... .

2. 📻 Listen to Carl telling Michelle what Tina told him. Carl told Michelle five lies. What were they?

4 Practice

Change the direct speech to reported speech.

a. "The children are going," she said.
b. "I have to leave tomorrow," he said.
c. "He can't see you until 4:00," his secretary said.
d. "They will be here tonight," his boss said.
e. "We need more milk," my father said.
f. "There's no school tomorrow," the children said.
g. "I've been to Disneyworld twice," she said.

5 Talk in Pairs

Ask your partner these questions, then report his/her answers to the class.

a. Can you dance very well?
b. Do you have any brothers or sisters?
c. Have you traveled to other countries?
d. Are you going to a party this weekend?
e. Do you like studying English?

Before You Read

1. Do you like amusement park rides? Why or why not?

2. What is a *bungee cord*? If you don't know, look it up in your dictionary.

1 Reading

Read the following article and choose the word to complete these statements.

a. You can probably find a bungee ride at a (circus/amusement park/playground).

b. A paraplegic is a person who cannot (walk/see/talk).

c. Adrenalin is (blood/fear/a chemical).

d. People ride the Ejection Seat (in pairs/alone/in groups).

Three Short Minutes to Eternity

Three minutes can be both the shortest and the longest period of time in your life.

"Impossible!" you say.

No, it's not impossible, because in those three minutes you will feel sure that your heart has stopped and that your stomach has jumped to your throat. You will feel the ultimate terror and the ultimate thrill. You will feel all of this in just three minutes.

The place to feel all these thrills is on the Ejection Seat, a bungee ride. However, before you line up for your ticket, it's important to read the warning at the entrance.

THE EJECTION SEAT

SAFETY FIRST!
WARNING!

DO NOT PARTICIPATE IF YOU:
- have had back or neck problems
- have heart problems
- have broken bones
- are pregnant
- have any other physical or medical problems

IT IS UP TO YOU TO MAKE THE RIGHT DECISION.

PLEASE USE YOUR COMMON SENSE!

What happens after you make the right decision? You and another person who has made the right decision are strapped into side-by-side chairs. You are then thrown 43 meters into the air (the height of a 14 storey building) at 100 km. per hour (4 times the force of gravity). You then spin wildly back down to earth where you will spend much more than three minutes trying to stop shaking.

What kind of people dare to fly up on a ride like that? Although all kinds of people of all ages go on the Ejection Seat, in general, more women than men take the risk. On at least one occasion, a paraplegic man went on it. He had always wanted to try something extremely exciting and dangerous. So, his legs were strapped underneath him, and up (and down) he went.

The bungee ride is not for everyone, but it can be the most thrilling ride you'll ever take.

2 Vocabulary Building DICT

1. Match the verbs with their definitions.

a. to line up
b. to throw
c. to strap
d. to dare
e. to take a risk

1. to do something dangerous
2. to be brave enough to do something
3. to send into the air
4. to wait in a line of people
5. to tie

2. Here are some verbs that indicate a particular kind of movement. Match each one with a diagram.

a. spin   b. jump   c. fly up   d. shake   e. roll

1.   2.   3.   4.   5.

3. Make a question with each verb. Ask your partner.

3 Listening

1. 📼 Listen to Tony Pyatt talk about his experience at the Edmonton shopping mall, in Canada.

2. Put the events in order.
a. Tony went ice skating.
b. Tony had lunch.
c. Tony went to the amusement park.
d. Tony went swimming.
e. Tony went to Marine Land.

4 Talk in Pairs or Groups

1. Do you like to go to amusement parks? Why or why not?

2. What is the most exciting ride you have ever been on? Describe why it was so exciting.

5 Writing

1. A concluding sentence sums up the ideas in your composition. What is the concluding sentence in the article in this unit?

2. Suggest a concluding sentence for each topic.
a. A day at an amusement park.
b. A unusual day in my life.

3. Write a letter to a friend about a special day you had recently. Begin like this:

> Your address
> Date

Dear ..... ,

Paragraph 1: Ask about your friend's health and activities.

Paragraph 2: Talk about how your day started. Talk about all the things that you did. Use some of the vocabulary you have learned in this course. Write a concluding sentence.

Paragraph 3: Say that you are looking forward to hearing from them. Express your good wishes.

> Your friend .....

At the Start

1. Have you ever been a tourist? Did you go to a tourist information center? What kinds of questions did you ask?

2. Read this interview with Tina Maxwell and find the silly questions that people have asked her.

1 Dictionary Work

1. Look up the pronunciation of these words in the dictionary: Greenwich Village statue museum thought concert

What is surprising about the pronunciation of each word? Check your pronunciation with your partner.

2. Look up *weather* and *whether*. Are they pronounced the same?

3. Words that are pronounced the same but have different meanings are called *homophones*. Write a homophone for each of the words below. Some have more than one.
pear bear clothes where would to I no by their you're hour it's here

Job Line

Tina Maxwell 30
New York City Tourist Information Center

What kinds of questions do visitors to New York ask you?
Absolutely anything. Well, one woman asked me whether the White House was open on Sundays. She was very upset when I told her that it was in Washington D.C. She thought that New York was the capital of the United States!

What do most people want to know?
They need information about hotels, trains, buses, the theaters, concerts, museums, all kinds of things. One man asked me if I remembered his brother. He couldn't believe that I don't remember all the people I speak to.

What is the strangest question you've heard?
There are so many it's hard to choose. The first day I worked here I talked to an Australian man. He asked if there were rooms available at the Statue of Liberty for that night. He thought it was a hotel! One woman asked me if she could drive to Greenwich Village in one day. She didn't know that it was right in New York City. Another couple asked me whether I had Arnold Schwarzenegger's telephone number. They wanted to invite him to dinner that night.

2 Spotlight

Study the structures below.

direct speech	reported speech
"**Do you have** Arnold Schwarzenegger's telephone number?" they asked. "**We want** to invite him to dinner **tonight**."	They asked me **whether I had** Arnold Schwarzenegger's telephone number. **They wanted** to invite him to dinner **that night**.
"**Can I** drive to Greenwich Village in one day?" she asked.	She asked me **if she could** drive to Greenwich Village in one day.
"**Did you see** my brother this morning?" he asked.	He asked **if I had seen** his brother that morning.

> ! Reported yes/no questions begin with *if* or *whether*.

> ! Reported yes/no questions use normal sentence word order.

3 Listening

⌨ Listen to these conversations and note the reported question in each one. Decide who asked the question.

4 Practice

1. Change the direct questions to reported questions.

a. "Are the children going?" she asked.
b. "Do I have to leave tomorrow?" he asked.
c. "Can you do me a favor?" my mother asked.
d. "Are they going out tonight?" his boss asked.
e. "Do we need more milk?" my father asked.
f. "Did you meet her?" the man asked.

2. Ask your classmates five funny yes/no questions. Then report some of the questions you were asked.

5 Talk in Pairs

Look at the pictures of these people. Decide what they have just said. Begin like this:
He has just told her that ..... .
She has just asked him if ..... .

1. Complete the following sentences with the correct form of one of the multi-word verbs from the list.

run out of   turn off   give up   clean up

blow up

a. After trying for a number of years, he finally ..... smoking.

b. Did you boys ..... the mess in the garage?

c. People still don't realize that we ..... water if we aren't careful with it.

d. Do you remember that terrible noise we heard last night? Well, some gas tanks ..... .

e. Please don't ..... the lights yet. I have to lock all the windows first.

2. Complete the following paragraph with the correct form of each verb. Use the present perfect, past, or past continuous.

I ^{1}..... with a terrible headache at 3 o'clock in
  _{wake up}
the morning. I ^{2}..... downstairs to get an
  _{go}
aspirin. While I ^{3}..... it in the cabinet, I suddenly
  _{look for}
^{4}..... a strange noise. I ^{5}..... around, but I ^{6}.....
_{hear}   _{turn}   _{not see}
anything. I ^{7}..... I ^{8}..... things, when I ^{9}..... the
  _{think} _{imagine}   _{hear}
same noise again. It ^{10}..... from the stairs. I ^{11}.....
  _{come}   _{be}
terrified, because my children ^{12}..... upstairs. I
  _{sleep}
^{13}..... my son's baseball bat, so I ^{14}..... it up and
_{see}   _{pick}
^{15}..... towards the stairs. A shadow ^{16}..... up the
_{go}   _{move}
stairs! But, nobody ^{17}..... there! I ^{18}..... the
  _{be}   _{follow}
shadow, but when I ^{19}..... to the top of the stairs,
  _{get}
it ^{20}..... . Since then, I ^{21}..... the same shadow
  _{disappear}   _{see}
three times. It always ^{22}..... at the top of the
  _{disappear}
stairs.

3. Complete the following sentences logically.

a. I'll go with you if ..... .

b. If we don't have to work tomorrow, ...

c. They'll win the award if ..... .

d. You'll understand if ..... .

e. If he doesn't come soon, ...

4.  Listen to this telephone conversation between Helen and Neil. Complete the conversation.

NEIL: Hi, Helen, how's it going?

HELEN: Pretty good, Neil, thanks.

NEIL: Helen, ^{1}..... very busy?

HELEN: No, I'm not very busy right now. What can I do for you?

NEIL: Well, I need some help. ^{2}.....another math test tomorrow, and I ^{3}..... anything.

HELEN: ^{4}..... your textbook and your notes?

NEIL: Well, I have my textbook, but I ^{5}..... my notes. But I ^{6}..... Pete's notes.

HELEN: O.K. ^{7}..... this afternoon about 5:00?

NEIL: I sure can, Helen! Thanks a lot.

5. Helen is telling her sister, Angie, about her conversation with Neil. Complete the conversation.

He said he needed help.

HELEN: Neil just called. He asked if [1]..... very busy.

ANGIE: What did you say?

HELEN: Well, I said that [2]..... very busy right now, and I asked [3]..... . He said that [4]..... . He said [5]..... another math test and [6]..... anything. I asked him [7]..... notes.

ANGIE: And?

HELEN: He said [8]....., but [9]..... notes.

ANGIE: That's typical! So what did you say ?

HELEN: Nothing, because he promised he [10]..... Pete's notes. I asked him [11]..... this afternoon at 5:00.

ANGIE: What did he say?

HELEN: He said [12]..... .

ANGIE: Well, I guess we'll see him this afternoon, then.

6. Rewrite the sentences that have separable multi-word verbs.

a. He's depressed because he broke up with his girlfriend.

b. It's time to get on the bus.

c. You have to fill out this form before you have your interview.

d. They threw out all the old letters.

7. Jake wanted to buy this old car. Lou said he would fix it for him.

Now look at the second picture and say what was done to the car. Use these verbs:

clean   paint   fix   change   put in

8. Write a good topic sentence and a good concluding sentence for the paragraph in 2.

Optional Exercises and Activities

Unit 1

1. Complete the sentences with the correct form of any verb that makes sense.

a. I ..... when she rang the doorbell.

b. While he ....., I was watching television.

c. First I ..... the clothes, then I ..... the soap. Finally, I ..... the washing machine.

d. We ..... when the bomb ..... .

e. He ..... when we ..... .

2. Answer these questions.

a. What were you doing when this class began?

b. What were your classmates doing last night?

c. What was your teacher doing yesterday at 5 p.m? (ask!)

Unit 2

1. Complete the following conversations using *(not) as...as* or the superlative of an adjective.

a. A: I don't believe it! That exam was really easy.

   B: I agree. It was ..... that last homework exercise.

b. A: Did you see the movie, *In the Darkness*?

   B: I sure did! It was absolutely horrible! Actually, I think it's ..... movie of the year.

c. A: Gosh, it's cold today.

   B: I don't think so. At least, it's ..... today ..... yesterday.

   A: Well, I think today is ..... day we've had so far.

2. Write these sentences in another way to mean the same thing.

Example:
My brother is older than my sister.
My sister is not as old as my brother.

a. The Ford is more expensive than the Volkswagen.

b. Two pounds of potatoes is the same price as a pound of rice.

c. I didn't get up as early today as I did yesterday.

3. 🔲 Listen to the following sentences. Notice the pronunciation of *as*.

a. She's as old as I am.

b. They're not as sweet as the other apples.

c. Are you as sleepy as I am?

d. That box isn't as big as this one.

e. My new watch isn't as good as my old one.

Now listen again and repeat.

4. Work with a partner. Look at this information about these new running shoes. Use the information to make up an ad. Present your ad to the class.

light, modern, designed for the future, available in various colors, incredible price.

Unit 3

1. Complete these sentences with tag questions.

a. You passed the exam, ... ?

b. The children aren't with you, ... ?

c. He doesn't like me, ... ?

d. It's a beautiful day, ... ?

e. You don't have any money, ... ?

2. Student A: Read this information about Ben. Find out if it's TRUE or FALSE by asking your partner tag questions. Then answer your partner's questions about Lorraine. Student B: Turn to page 68.

Ben:

born in 1967
graduated from Ohio State University
played football at university
lives in Columbus, Ohio
accountant
married
three children

Lorraine:

born in London
moved to the United States in 1975
attended New York University
studied architecture
lives in San Francisco, California
divorced
one child

Unit 4

1. Answer these questions using *too* or *enough*.

a. Can you swim a kilometer?

b. Can you wear size six shoes?

c. Can you stay up late at night?

d. Can you walk to school?

2. Find the word that doesn't fit.

a. sleeping bag   chair   bed   television

b. can   box   bag   fork

c. heater   refrigerator   stove   iron

d. compass   map   the sun   match

e. water   food   car   air

3. Work in a small group. You have crashed on the moon. You have to walk 250 kilometers to the space station. Look at the list of things to take below and write number 1 for the most important, up to number 15 for the least important.

matches
dried food
20 meters of rope
small heater
two guns
12 packages of dried milk
2 100-pound tanks of oxygen
compass
20 gallons of water
first-aid kit
star map
life raft
solar-powered 2-way radio
signal flares

Unit 5

1. **DICT** Student A: Write definitions for the following subjects or work areas, or people. Read your definitions to your partner. Your partner guesses who or what you are defining. Student B: Turn to page 68.

Example:
plumber   A: *someone who fixes water pipes in your house.*
       B: *a plumber*

a. mathematician

b. chemistry

c. carpenter

2. Write a paragraph about Samuel Morse. Connect the sentences with adverbs of sequence when possible.

1791 – Born in Massachusetts, U.S.A.
1810 – Studies art in England.
1826 – Sets up the National Academy of Design in N.Y.
1830 – Starts experiment using electricity to send messages.
1844 – The U.S. government choses his system as the official telegraph system.

3. 🎧 Listen to the following sentences. Which word has the most stress?

a. They always do their homework.

    They always do their homework.

b. He rarely misses class.

    He rarely misses class.

c. She never gets up early.

    She never gets up early.

Is the meaning the same in each pair of sentences?

Now listen again and repeat the sentences.

Unit 6

1. Each of these statements is FALSE. Change the modal and make them TRUE.

a. The sun might rise in the East tomorrow.

b. Good students shouldn't get to class on time.

c. Everyone in your class will learn to speak English perfectly.

d. Horses won't run faster than cars.

e. People from outer space will visit Earth next month.

f. Children can't obey their parents.

2. Student A: Read your problem to your partner. He or she will give you some advice. Student B: Turn to page 68.

a. Your best friend is going to run away and get married. She/He is only 17. You are the only person that knows.

b. You just saw your girl/boyfriend with someone else. He/She promised that they wouldn't go out with anyone else.

Unit 7

1. DICT Find the word on the right that contains the same sound as the letter or letters in bold in the word on the left.

a. mea**s**ure	Asia	surprise	cookies
b. lau**gh**	neighbor	fish	heat
c. w**ei**gh	rough	hello	great
d. **ph**armacy	pet	high	tough
e. **s**ure	she	sue	soup

2. Write questions for these answers.

a. ..... ? Yes, I've visited Spain and England.

b. ..... ? No, I haven't. I've never had time to learn.

c. ..... ? Yes, I have. It was great.

d. ..... ? No, I haven't, but I'd like to do it some day.

e. ..... ? Yes, I have. He's my favorite actor.

3. Write a series of *I have...* sentences about yourself. Don't write your name. The teacher will read out the sentences and your classmates will try to guess who you are.

Unit 8

1. DICT Find the synonyms by matching the columns.

a. terrified	**1.** drive away
b. protection	**2.** a little
c. device	**3.** very strong
d. a bit	**4.** very frightened
e. powerful	**5.** instrument
f. repel	**6.** work
g. operate	**7.** covering

2. Use one of the words in 1 in the following sentences. Put the verbs in the correct form.

a. I don't know how to ..... this camera.

b. She's ..... tired today.

c. That smell ..... insects.

d. Tigers are ..... animals.

e. After he fell in the lake, he was ..... of the water.

3. Complete the following sentences.

a. I did my homework before ..... .

b. While ..... , we finished making lunch.

c. After ..... , they went out for dinner.

d. We were at the shopping center when ..... .

e. While she was reading, ...

f. Before he went into the classroom, ...

g. I didn't want to drive the car after ..... .

h. When they left the house, ...

4. 🖭 Read the following words and listen to the pronunciation.

Did you   Can't you

Notice that a final *d* is pronounced /j/, and a final *t* is pronounced /ch/ when they are followed by *you*.

Listen again and repeat.

Now listen to the following sentences and notice where the last sound of a word changes.

a. What are the most famous movies that you've worked on?

b. Why don't you help me?

c. Where did you study English this year?

d. When did your class get out?

Unit 9

1. Complete the sentences with *for* or *since*.

a. I've lived in the same house ..... my whole life.

b. They've been married ..... 1969.

c. He's been here ..... three weeks.

d. They've been visiting ..... the beginning of summer.

e. She's been sick ..... Tuesday.

2. Look at the list and say what Pablo *has done* and *hasn't done* today.

TO DO

X go grocery shopping
call dentist
pay credit card bill
X pick up dry cleaning
order concert tickets
make plane reservations
X take the car to the mechanic

3. Student A: You are the manager of ABC Taxi company. You are interviewing people to be taxi drivers. Ask Student B for this information. Student B: Turn to page 68.

Name --
Address --
How long? -------------- Age ----------------
Driver's license yes/no How long? -------

EDUCATION
High school ----------------------------------
year of graduation ----------------------------
College --
year of graduation ----------------------------

WORK EXPERIENCE

"Johnson for Senator"

Unit 10

1. Look at this political speech. It has many errors. Rewrite it correctly.

Before you decide voting for my opponent, I think you should listen to some facts. He says that he wants to fixing the schools but I can't help to notice that he always votes against education laws. He says the we need building a new hospital but he avoids to paying taxes when he can. He has agreed to tells the truth but he keeps on lie.

2. DICT Look up these verbs in the dictionary. Do they take infinitives or gerunds? Write a sentence for each one.

delay deserve dread fail intend miss regret

3. 🔊 The pronunciation of the word *to* often changes in phrases such as *want to, need to, have to, hate to, like to.* Listen carefully and compare the two pronunciations. How is the second one different?

a. I want to go with you.

b. They need to study.

c. We have to leave now.

d. You hate to exercise.

e. I like to get up early.

Listen again and repeat the normal pronunciation.

Unit 11

1. DICT Fill in the blanks. Use the correct form of the verb, or change the verb to an adjective as required.

a. I don't like to read the paper. The news is always so ..... !
   depress

b. They were making noise again this morning and it really ..... me.
   irritate

c. I think physics is such a ..... subject.
   confuse

d. My little brother had a very ..... experience
   frighten
   yesterday.

e. My parents ..... me on our vacation.
   amaze
   They were so full of energy!

f. I'm sorry I ..... you last night. I forgot my
   disturb
   keys.

g. Well, it looks like these documents ..... all
   satisfy
   the requirements.

h. The president gave a very ..... speech on TV
   inspire
   last night.

2. Combine the sentences with *and, but* or *so.*

a. I forgot my books at school. I didn't do my homework.

b. We went to the ocean for our vacation. We had a wonderful time.

c. Our teacher was sick yesterday. We didn't have class.

d. The weather was cloudy and cool. My friends and I went swimming anyway.

e. I think it's crazy. I love it.

3. Think of a noise. Fill in the information.

What time of day or night you can hear it:
How often you can hear it:
Where you can hear it:
How it makes you feel:

Now have your partner guess what the noise is.

4. 🔊 Read and listen to the following *-ing* adjectives. Notice where the stressed syllable is in each one.

a. interesting

b. entertaining

c. frustrating

d. boring

e. annoying

Now listen again and repeat the words.

Unit 12

1. Complete the sentences with *already* or *yet.*

a. She hasn't studied ..... .

b. I've ..... finished my work.

c. The children haven't come back ..... .

d. Have you finished the exam ..... ?

2. Look at this room. Say what Sylvia has *already* done and what she hasn't done *yet*.

cleared the table
eaten dinner
emptied the garbage
fed the cat
put away the milk
swept the floor
washed the dishes

3. Play grammar tic-tac-toe with a partner. One person is X and the other is O. Make a sentence using one of the words in the grid. If the sentence is correct, put an X or an O over the word. If you think your partner is wrong, ask your teacher. The first person to get three X's or O's in a line wins.

yet	eaten	since
are	written	already
for	they	taught

seen	gone	she
is	already	hugged
done	yet	been

Unit 13

1. Write about how these people feel and say what you think happened to make them feel that way.

Example:
Sandra looks bored. I think she is listening to a boring lecture.

a. Sandra　　**b.** Cliff　　**c.** Harry　　**d.** Claudia　　**e.** Lila

2. Ask your partner questions to complete these sentences.

a. ..... often feels bored when ..... .

b. He/She gets excited when ..... .

c. He/She thinks the most confusing thing about English is ..... .

d. He/She was amazed when ..... .

e. He/She thinks the most frightening thing that ever happened to her/him was when ..... .

Unit 14

1. Fill in the blanks with the correct adjective or its opposite.

> patient   interested   unselfish   organized
> satisfactory   reliable

I'm afraid I have to speak to you very seriously, Mr. Thornton. Recently your work has been very [1]..... . In general, you are [2]..... . Sometimes your performance is excellent, and then suddenly it is just the opposite. Your office is always [3]..... . I don't know how you can find anything in there. I know you have your good qualities as well, Mr. Thornton. I've noticed that you are [4]..... ; you are always willing to help someone in difficulties. You are also very [5]..... with people who can't understand a particular situation quickly. Perhaps the problem is that you have become [6]..... in your work, Mr. Thornton. What do you think?

2. Read the following paragraph. Rewrite it, using periods, commas and capital letters where necessary.

i grew up as an only child i think that most of the time i was pretty happy but i felt that i had one big disadvantage i didn't know how to talk to boys my father was rarely at home because he was a salesman for a medical laboratory and he had to travel a lot my mother and i had some good times together but i didn't have enough confidence to tell her about my problem with boys i tried to solve my problem by staying away from boys but this became more and more difficult as my girl friends started inviting boys to their parties

Unit 15

1. Find the errors and correct them.

a. We lived here since 1975.

b. They hid when they hear the noise.

c. I cooked when I saw the ghost.

d. She has gone there last week.

e. My brother has worked there since ten years.

f. I slept when the telephone woke me up.

2. Rewrite this paragraph about yourself. Use the correct form of the verb, another verb or the necessary information.

I ..... born in ..... in ..... . I ..... school when I was ..... years old.

(be)   (year)   (place) (start)   (age)

I ..... school very much because ..... . I ..... primary school/high

(not) like   (reason) (finish)

school/college in ..... . Then I ..... . For the past ..... years/months I

(year)   (verb phrase)   (number)

..... in ..... . I ..... , but I would like to one day.

live (place)   never + (verb phrase)

3. Write questions for the answers.

a. ..... ? I was playing the piano.

b. ..... ? Yes, I have.

c. ..... ? I went with my mother.

d. .... ? He went to Detroit.

e. ..... ? You were sleeping.

Unit 16

1. Match the two halves of these sentences.

a. if Susan goes to the store   **1.** Dave is going to learn to drive

b. John might be angry   **2.** if she has time

c. Joe should pay attention   **3.** she can buy us some milk

d. if I buy a new car   **4.** if he finds out you lied

e. Paula will exercise today   **5.** if you tell him it's important

Now rewrite the sentences with correct punctuation.

2. Write a chain of circumstances that lead to each result.

a. If ..... and then ..... , you'll get sick.

b. If ..... and then ..... , you'll be able to take a long vacation.

c. If ..... and then ..... , she'll marry you!

Unit 17

1. `DICT` Match the verbs with the prepositions. Make as many pairs as you can.

keep sign give		in on up off out
put get call fill		back

2. `DICT` Now make a sentence with each multi-word verb above. Use the dictionary to help you.

3. Student A: You have half of a story. Student B has the other half. Listen to Student B's sentences and put the story together, without looking at Student B's page. Student B: Look at page 69.

Sentence 1:
Last night there was a big fire at the gas station across the street from my house.

The fire fighters came quickly but the fire kept on spreading. Finally, after 30 minutes they were able to put out the fire. The attendant threw water on the flames.
A woman in a car told him to turn off the water.

Unit 18

1. Exchange the composition you wrote in the unit with your partner. Make notes about the following points:

a. what was the same.

c. what you liked.

b. what was different.

d. what you didn't like.

Now share your ideas with your partner.

2. Write a topic sentence for each of the following paragraphs.

a. Everything seemed perfect. Marilyn's mother made us a delicious breakfast to give us a good start. We said goodbye and got in the car, John and I in the front, and Marilyn stretched out in the back. John was a good driver, and soon we were on the winding highway going into the mountains. Suddenly, a truck came flying around a curve, and headed straight towards us.

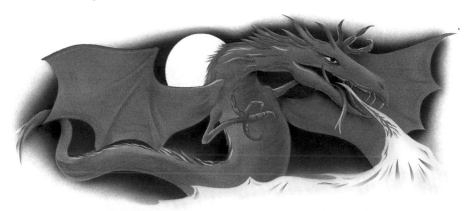

b. In some countries, the dragon was depicted as an evil monster, because he represented the struggle between good and evil. In other countries, such as China, however, the dragon was responsible for bringing rain, and rain dances were performed in his honor. The European dragon was based on the python snake. Some dragons had wings, and some breathed fire.

3. **DICT** Write definitions for the following words.

Example:
rain dance – a dance performed to bring rain.

a. washing machine

b. intelligence test

c. CD player

d. traveler's check

e. shoe laces

Unit 19

1. Student A: Write the sentences that Student B tells you. Then read your sentences to Student B. Finally, change the passive voice to active voice and the active voice to passive voice. Student B: turn to page 69.

a. One hundred years ago, many things were made by hand.

b. I didn't write this letter, Philip did.

c. The car was stolen and sold by a gang of thieves.

2. Find the errors and correct them.

a. The children given their presents.

b. He was died in the 1916.

c. The baby was borned yesterday.

d. He weren't told the truth.

e. The fire was put down by the afternoon.

f. I was call by the police.

g. In the past, animals were using to plow fields.

h. All the food were eaten by the time we arrived.

3. Look at the statement below. Write the things that happened because this event took place. Make as many passive voice sentences as you can, but not all your sentences need to be in the passive voice.

Last month there was a big campaign to clean up the city.

Example:
Trees were planted.

Unit 20

1. Change these quotations (direct speech) to reported speech.

a. Bill said, "I live with my mother."

b. "We've been here for three years," said Marta.

c. The teacher said "We will have an exam tomorrow."

d. "There are enough chairs here," said Karen.

e. "He gave me the book," said Diana.

f. "I can't do this," Sally said.

g. "We worked really hard," the students said.

h. Paul said, "They've fixed the phone."

2. Student A: You have half of a conversation. Student B has the other half. Change your half to direct speech and put the conversation together. Student B: turn to page 69.

She said that she had decided to drop out.
She said that she couldn't pay a tutor.
She said that she had failed almost every test.
Anne told Tyler that math class was difficult for her.

Unit 21

1. Fill the blanks with the correct form of the following verbs.

throw dive take risks start rush

understand spin see dare

Many people have found that the ocean is a beautiful but powerful force of nature. Strong swimmers who [1]..... in the ocean have discovered that they are not strong at all. My friend, Andrew, [2]..... this through an almost tragic experience last summer.

Andrew and a friend [3]..... into the waves near the shore when his friend [4]..... him to swim to a large rock a distance from the shore. Andrew [5]..... swimming towards the rock, but after a few minutes, a wave [6]..... him, and [7]..... him around and around. Several swimmers [8]..... what was happening, and they [9]..... to save him.

2. Write a good concluding sentence for the story above.

3. Read the composition your partner wrote and say:

a. what you found most exciting.

b. what activities don't interest you.

c. what activities you have never done.

4. 📼 Listen to these sentences from the reading.

It's up to you.
It's not impossible.

Which words are run together?

In each of the following sentences, some words are run together. Listen and say which ones.

a. It's important to read the warning.

b. People of all ages go.

c. A paraplegic man went on it.

d. What kind of people dare to fly up on a ride like that?

e. Up and down he went.

Now listen again and repeat each sentence.

Unit 22

1. Student A: You have some questions and some answers. Student B will ask you his or her questions in reported speech. Find the correct answer, change it to reported speech and report it to Student B. Then read him or her your questions in reported speech. Student B: turn to page 69.

"Are you busy tonight?" Chris asked Kim.

"I'm sorry, I can't," Chris said.

"How about Saturday?" Chris asked.

"I'm tired of movies," Chris said.

2. Find the word in the list on the right that contains the same sound as the letter/s in bold in the word on the left.

a. concert	shoe	zoo	sue
b. museum	shoe	zoo	sue
c. canoe	knew	know	snowy
d. meet	could	teacher	cool
e. southern	south	bottom	but
f. could	cold	foot	can't

Optional Exercises and Activities – Student B

Unit 3

2. Student B: Read this information about Ben. Answer your partner's questions. Then read the information about Lorraine and ask your partner about her.

Ben:

born in 1970
graduated from Ohio State University
played soccer at university
lives in Cleveland, Ohio
accountant
married
two children

Lorraine:

born in London
moved to the United States in 1978
attended New York University
studied architecture
lives in Seattle, Washington
married
one child

Unit 5

2. DICT Student B: Write definitions for the following subjects or work areas, or people. Read your definitions to your partner. Your partner guesses who or what you are defining.

Example:
plumber A: *someone who fixes water pipes in your house.*
         B: *a plumber*

a. politics

b. magician

c. therapist

Unit 6

1. Student B: Read your problems to your partner. He or she will give you some advice.

a. You have just been offered a great job but friends tell you that your new employer is not honest. You really need the work.

b. You wake up and hear noises downstairs. You are alone in the house but you're sure that someone broke in.

Unit 9

3. Student B: you are applying for a job as a taxi driver. Here is the information to answer Student A's questions.

Name Adrian Baker
Address 227 Maple Avenue
How long? 2 years   **Age** 20
Driver's license yes/no   **How long?** 4 years

EDUCATION
High school Valley High School
year of graduation 1993
College State College
year of graduation still attending

WORK EXPERIENCE
Bus driver June 1993 – September 1993 Valley summer camp
Library attendant State College September 1993 – present

Unit 17

3. Student B: You have half of a story. Student A has the other half. Listen to Student A's sentences and put the story together, without looking at Student A's page.

#1 Last night there was a big fire at the gas station across the street from my house.

Someone was smoking a cigarette and suddenly a car burst into flames.
She called up the fire department on her car phone.
They were afraid that the gas tanks were going to blow up.
However, you can't put out a gas fire with water.

Unit 19

1. Student B: Read your sentences to Student A. He or she will write them. Then, write the sentences that Student A tells you. Finally, change the passive voice to active voice and the active voice to passive voice.

a. A lot of money was made by that company and a lots of people got jobs.

b. He fixed the computer and returned it the next day.

c. The book wasn't borrowed by me, it was borrowed by Tim.

Unit 20

2. Student B: You have half of a conversation. Student A has the other half. Change your half to direct speech and put the conversation together:

He said it was difficult for him too.
He said that she would be sorry if she dropped out.
He said that they could get a tutor together.
He said that he had bad grades too.

Unit 22

1. Student B: You have some questions and some answers. Student A will ask you his or her questions in reported speech. Find the correct answer, change it to reported speech and report it to Student A. Then read him or her your questions in reported speech.

"Yes, I am," Kim said.

"Do you want to go out tomorrow night?" Kim asked.

"That sounds good," Kim said.

"Should we go to a movie?" Kim asked.

Quiz Answers

Unit 13 – At the Start

YOUR SCORE
For each answer, count the number shown below.

1.	a. 1	b. 2	c. 3
2.	a. 3	b. 2	c. 1
3.	a. 1	b. 2	c. 3
4.	a. 3	b. 2	c. 1
5.	a. 1	b. 3	c. 2

Now total your answers and see how you score!

13-15
Well, you certainly aren't boring! You are probably an interesting, exciting person — the kind a lot of people would like to know.

10-12
You're interested in things but are a little nervous. Make your life more exciting. Try something new!

5-9
You're bored with life and you may be boring to others. Wake up! There are a lot of fascinating things to do!

Dictionary

This dictionary is a 1000-word sample from the Longman Learner's Dictionary of American English. The following chart is a modified version of the International Phonetic Alphabet. These characters are used to represent the pronunciation of the words listed in the dictionary.

Vowels

i	beat	ɑɪ	by
ɪ	bit	ɑʊ	bound
e	bait	ɔɪ	boy
ɛ	bet	ɪu	few
æ	bat	ɚr	burn
ɑ	box	ɪər	beer
ɔ	bought	ɛər	bare
o	boat	ʊər	tour
ʊ	book	ɪuər	cure
u	boot	ɑɪər	fire
ʌ	but		
ə	banana		

Consonants

p	pan	s	sip
b	ban	z	zip
t	tip	ʃ	ship
d	dip	ʒ	measure
k	cap	m	sum
g	gap	n	sun
tʃ	church	ŋ	sung
dʒ	judge	r	rot
f	fan	l	lot
v	van	w	wet
θ	thin	y	yet
ð	then		

The grammar codes used in this dictionary are:

[S] noun that is singular only   [C] countable noun
[U] uncountable noun   [I] intransitive verb
[P] noun that is plural only   [T] transitive verb

The abbreviations used in this dictionary are:

adj	adjective	*masc*	masculine
adv	adverb	*n*	noun
aux	auxiliary	*phr v*	phrasal (multi-word) verb
cap	capitalized	*pl*	plural
conj	conjunction	*prep*	preposition
e.g.	for example	*pres*	present
esp	especially	*pron*	pronoun
etc	etcetera - and so on	*sing*	singular
fem	feminine	*sl*	slang
fml	formal	*usu*	usually
infml	informal	*v*	verb
interj	interjection		

ab·so·lute·ly /ˌæbsəˈlutlɪ/ *adv* **1** completely **2** certainly: 'Do you think so?' 'Absolutely!'

a·chieve /əˈtʃiv/ *v* [T] **1** finish successfully **2** get by effort

ac·me /ˈækmi/ *n* [U] highest point: *the acme of perfection*

act /ækt/ *v* **1** do something **2** perform in a play or film ♦ *n* something that one has done: *a kind act*

ad /æd/ *n infml* advertisement

add /æd/ *v* **1** *v* [T] put with something else: *add a name to the list* **2** *v* [I/T] join (numbers) together

add to *phr v* [T] increase: *His absence added to our difficulties.*

ad·min·is·tra·tion /ədˌmɪnəˈstreɪʃən/ *n* [U] management or direction of a business, government, etc.

ad·mire /ədˈmɑɪər/ *v* [T] regard with pleasure; have a good opinion of **admiring** *adj* **admirer** *n* **admiration** /ˌædməˈreʃən/ *n* [U] feeling of pleasure and respect

ad·o·les·cent /ˌædəlˈɛsənt/ *adj, n* (of) a boy or girl who is growing up ~**cence** *n* [S;U]

ad·van·tage /ədˈvæntɪdʒ/ *n* [C] something that may help one to be successful **take advantage of**: make use of somebody, as by deceiving them, for one's own benefit

ad·vice /ədˈvɑɪs/ *n* [U] opinion given to someone about what to do

ad·vise /ədˈvɑɪz/ *v* [T] **1** give advice to **2** [(of)] *fml* inform: *Please advise me of the cost.* **adviser** also **advisor** *n* **advisable** *adj* sensible

aer·o·bics /ɛəˈrobɪks/ *n* [U] active physical exercise done to strengthen the heart and lungs

af·ter /ˈæftər/ *prep, conj* **1** later than: *after breakfast | after you leave* **2** following: *Your name comes after mine in the list.*

a·gainst /əˈgɛnst/ *prep* **1** in the direction of and meeting or touching: *against the windows* **2** in opposition to; not in favour of: *He voted against me.*

a·gree /əˈgri/ *v* **1** *v* [I/T +to-v] share the same opinion; say 'yes': *I agree with you. | We agreed to go home.* **2** *v* [I] (of statements, etc.) be the same; match ~**able** *adj* pleasant ~**ably** *adv* ~**ment** *n*

air /ɛər/ *n* **1** [U] mixture of gases that we breathe **2** [U] space above the ground: *travel by air*

aisle /ɑɪl/ *n* passage between seats in a church, theater, etc.

al·bum /ˈælbəm/ *n* book for sticking photographs, etc. into

al·read·y /ɔlˈrɛdi/ *adv* **1** by or before an expected time: *Are you leaving already?* **2** before now: *I've seen the film twice already.*

a·maze /əˈmez/ *v* [T] fill with great surprise: *I was amazed to hear the news. | an amazing film* ~**ment** *n* [U] **amazingly** *adv*

a·muse·ment park /əˈmyuzmənt pɑrk/ *n* park with things to do and machines to ride on

and /ənd, ən; *strong* ænd/ *conj* **1** as well as: *John and Sally* **2** then; therefore: *Water the seeds and they will grow.*

an·ger /ˈæŋgər/ *n* [U] fierce displeasure and annoyance **angry** /-gri/ *adj* full of anger

an·ni·ver·sa·ry /ˌænəˈvɚsəri/ *n* day that is an exact number of years after something happened

an·noy /əˈnɔɪ/ *v* [T] make a little angry; cause trouble to: *an annoying delay* ~**ance** *n* [C;U] ~**ing** *adj*

ap·pear /əˈpɪər/ *v* [I] **1** come into sight **2** seem: *He appears to be angry.*

ap·ply /əˈplɑɪ/ *v* [T] request officially: *apply for a job*

ar·rest /əˈrɛst/ *v* [T] **1** seize by the power of the law **2** stop (a process) ♦ *n* [C;U] act of arresting

ar·rive /əˈrɑɪv/ *v* [I] **1** reach a place: *arrive home* **2** happen; come: *The day arrived.*

as /æz/ *adv, prep* (used in comparisons): *He's as old as me.*

A·sia /ˈeʒə/ *n* the land east of Europe, west of the Pacific Ocean, and north of the Indian Ocean

as·ton·ish /əˈstɑnɪʃ/ *v* [T] surprise greatly: *His rudeness astonished me.* ~**ment** *n* [U]

as·tound /əˈstaʊnd/ *v* [T] shock with surprise

at·ten·tive /əˈtɛntɪv/ *adj* **1** listening carefully **2** politely helpful ~**ly** *adv* ~**ness** *n* [U]

au·di·ence /ˈɔdiəns/ *n* people listening to or watching a performance

a·vai·la·ble /əˈveləbəl/ *adj* able to be gotten, used, etc.: *Those shoes are not available in your size.* ~**bility** /əˌveləˈbɪləti/ *n* [U]

a·void /əˈvɔɪd/ *v* [T +v-ing] keep away from, esp. on purpose ~**able** *adj* ~**ance** *n* [U]

a·way /əˈwe/ *adv* to or at another place: *Go away! | She lives 3 miles away.*

bal·loon /bəˈlun/ *n* small rubber bag that can be blown up with gas or air and used as a toy

bare /bɛər/ *adj* **1** without clothes or covering **2** with nothing added: *the bare facts* **3** empty: *a room bare of furniture* ~**ly** *adv* only just

be /bɪ; *strong* bi/ *v* **am/is/are; was/were** to show something exists; *past p.* **been**; *pres. p.* **being**; *v aux*: *I am/was reading. |We are/were invited.*

bean /bin/ *n* seed of any of various plants, esp. used as food: *coffee beans*

bear¹ /bɛər/ *n* large, heavy furry animal that eats meat, fruit, and insects

bear² *v* [T] **bore** /bɔr/ **borne** /bɔrn/ **1** carry **2** support (a weight) **3** have; show **4** suffer or accept (something unpleasant) without complaining

be·come /bɪˈkʌm/ *v* **became, become** begin to be: *become king | become warmer*

be·gin /bɪˈgɪn/ *v* [I/T] **began** /bɪˈgæn/, **begun** /bɪˈgʌn/ start; take the first step ~**ner** *n* person starting to learn ~**ning** *n* [C;U] starting point

be·lieve /bɪˈliv/ *v* [T] consider to be true **believable** *adj*

bet /bɛt/ *n* **1** agreement to risk money on a future event **2** sum of money risked in this way ♦ *v* [I/T] **bet** or **betted**; *pres. p.* **betting 1** risk (money) on a race, etc. **2** *infml* be sure: *I bet he's angry!*

bet·ter-off /ˌbɛtər ˈɔf/ *adj* **1** richer **2** luckier

bill·board /ˈbɪlbɔrd/ *n* a large board outdoors used for advertisements

bil·lion /ˈbɪlyən/ *n* billion, billions 1,000,000,000

bi·ol·o·gy /bɑɪˈɑlədʒi/ *n* [U] scientific study of living things ~**gist** *n* ~**gical** /ˌbɑɪəˈlɑdʒɪkəl/ *adj*

bit /bɪt/ *n* **1** small piece **2** short time: *a bit longer* **3** small amount: *a bit tired*

blow up /blo ˈʌp/ *phr v* [I/T] **1** explode **2** fill with air as a balloon

bomb /bɑm/ *n* **1** [C] container filled with explosive ♦ *v* [T] attack with bombs ~**proof** *adj* giving protection against bombs

boot /but/ *n* heavy shoe that comes up over the ankle

bore /bɔr/ *v* [T] make (someone) tired or uninterested **bored** *adj* **boring** *adj*

bot·tom /ˈbɑtəm/ *n* lowest part or level

bound /baʊnd/ *adj* going to (a place): *bound for home*

brave /brev/ *adj* ready to meet pain or danger; fearless

break /brek/ *v* **broke** /brok/, **broken** /ˈbrokən/ **1** [I/T] separate suddenly into parts: *to break a window* **2** *v* [I/T] make or become useless as a result of damage: *a broken watch* **3** *v* [T] disobey; not keep: *break a promise/an appointment* **4** *v* [I/T] interrupt; stop: *break the silenc*

break up with *phr v* [T] end one's friendship or romance with

break with *phr v* [T] end one's connection with

build /bɪld/ *v* [I/T] **built** /bɪlt/ make by putting pieces together: *build houses/ships* ~**ing** *n* thing with a roof and walls; house, etc.

bul·let /ˈbʊlɪt/ *n* small piece of lead fired from a gun ~**proof** *adj* giving protection against bullets

bun·gee cord /ˈbʌndʒi ˌkɔrd/ *n* elastic rope tied to one's body when making a jump from a very high place, for pleasure

burn /bɜrn/ *v* **burnt** /bɜnt, bɜrnt/ **1** *v* [I] be on fire: *a burning match/house* **2** *v* [T] damage or destroy by fire

burst into /ˌbɜrst ˈɪntʊ/ *phr v* [T] **1** enter quickly or suddenly **2** start a new state suddenly: *The house burst into flames. He burst into song.*

bus /bʌs/ *n* large motor vehicle for carrying passengers

but /bət; *strong* bʌt/ *conj* **1** rather; instead: *not one, but two* **2** yet at the same time; however: *I want to go, but I can't.*

buy /baɪ/ *v* [I/T] **bought** /bɔt/ obtain by paying money

by /baɪ/ *prep, adv* **1** beside; near: *Sit by me.* **2** through; using: *enter by the door* | *travel by car* **3** past: *He walked by (me) without speaking.* **4** before: *Do it by tomorrow.* **5** (shows who or what does something): *a play by Shakespeare*

caf·e /kæˈfe/ *n* small restaurant serving light meals and drinks

caf·feine /ˈkæfin/ *n* [U] substance found in coffee and tea, which keeps one awake

cal·cu·la·ble /ˈkælkyələbəl/ *adj* able to be measured

call¹ /kɔl/ *v* **1** *v* [I/T] speak or say loudly **2** *v* [T] name: *We'll call the baby Jean.* **3** *v* [T] tell to come: *Call a doctor!* **4** *v* [I/T] contact with a telephone **5** *v* [T] say publicly that something is to happen: *call a meeting/an election/a strike* **6** *v* [T] say to be: *She called me a coward.* **8** *v* [T] waken: *Please call me at 7.*

call² *n* **1** shout; cry **2** telephone conversation **3** short visit

call back *phr v* [I/T] return a telephone call

call in *phr v* [T] ask to come: *call the doctor in*

call off *phr v* [T] **1** decide not to have (a planned event) **2** tell to keep away: *Call off your dog!*

call on *phr v* [T] ask to do something

call out *phr v* [T] speak or say loudly; shout

call up *phr v* [T] **1** telephone **2** order to join the armed forces

camp /kæmp/ *n* [C;U] place where people live in tents or huts for a short time ♦ *v* [I] set up or live in a camp: *We camp in the mountains every summer.*

campstove /ˈkæmpstov/ *n* small stove for use when camping

can¹ /kən; *strong* kæn/ *v aux* **1** be able to: *Can you swim?* **2** be allowed to; may: *You can go home now.*

can² *n* metal container for foods or liquids ♦ *v* [T] put in a can ~**ned** *adj* placed, sold etc. in a can

ca·noe /kəˈnu/ *n* light boat moved by a paddle

can't /kænt/ *v short for:* can not: *I can't come tonight.*

cap·i·tal /ˈkæpətl/ *n* **1** town where the center of government is **2** money used to start a business **3** letter in its large form; A, B, C, etc.

ca·reer /kəˈrɪər/ *n* **1** profession **2** general course of a person's life

care·ful /ˈkɛərfəl/ *adj* paying attention; taking care ~**ly** *adv*

car·pen·ter /ˈkɑrpəntər/ *n* person who makes wooden objects

car·ry /ˈkæri/ *v* [T] **1** move while supporting; have with one: *carry a gun* | *carry a child on one's back* **2** take from one place to another: *Pipes carry oil across the desert.*

case /kes/ *n* large box or container: *a packing case* | *a suitcase*

catch on /kætʃ ˈɑn/ *phr v* [I] **1** become popular **2** understand: *She catches on quickly.*

cause /kɔz/ *n* **1** [C;U] thing that produces a result: *the cause of the accident* **2** [U] reason: *no cause for complaint* ♦ *v* [T] be the cause of: *to cause trouble*

ce·re·al /ˈsɪəriəl/ *n* [C;U] breakfast food made from grain

change /tʃendʒ/ *v* **1** *v* [I/T] make or become different: *change the subject* | *water changed into ice* **2** *v* [T] give and receive in return: *change a library book* **3** *v* [I/T] leave and enter (different vehicles): *change (trains) at Chicago* **4** **change one's mind** form a new opinion ♦ *n* **1** money returned when something bought costs less than the amount paid **2** coins or notes of low value

chase /tʃes/ *v* [I/T] follow rapidly, in order to catch or drive away ♦ *n* **1** chasing something or someone **2** **give chase** chase someone

check /tʃek/ *n* **1** [C] examination to make sure something is correct **2** [S;U] stop; control: *keep the disease in check* **3** [C;U] pattern of squares **4** [C] restaurant bill **5** [C] written order to a bank to pay money **6** [C] mark (✓) put against an answer to show that it is correct or next to a name to show the person is present ♦ *v* [I/T] examine; make sure: *check a letter for spelling mistakes*

chem·ist /ˈkɛmɪst/ *n* scientist specializing in chemistry

chem·is·try /ˈkɛməstri/ *n* [U] science of natural substances and how they combine and behave

choc·o·late /ˈtʃɔklɪt/ *n* **1** [U] solid brown substance eaten as candy **2** [C] small candy covered with this **3** [U] hot drink made from this ♦ *adj* dark brown

choose /tʃuz/ *v* [I/T] **chose** /tʃoz/, **chosen** /ˈtʃozən/ decide on one out of many options: *choose a cake* | *choose where to go*

chore /tʃɔr/ *n* piece of regular or dull work

cir·cus /ˈsɜrkəs/ *n* performance of skill and daring by a group of people and animals

clean /klin/ *adj* not dirty ♦ *v* [T] make clean

clean up *phr v* [I/T] **1** clean **2** put things in their proper place

clear /klɪər/ *adj* **1** easy to see through **2** free of marks, obstacles, etc ♦ *v* [I/T] make or become clear

clear up *phr v* **1** *v* [T] explain: *clear up the mystery* **2** *v* [I/T] clean up

close¹ /kloz/ *v* **1** *v* [I/T] shut: *close one's eyes* | *When does the store close?* **2** *v* [T] bring to an end: *close a bank account*

close² /klos/ *adj* **1** near: *close to the stores* | *a close friend* **2** thorough: *close inspection*

close down *phr v* [I/T] (of a factory, etc.) stop operating **closedown** /ˈklozdaʊn/ *n*

clothes /kloz, kloðz/ *n* [P] things to cover the body; garments

clo·ver /ˈklovər/ *n* [C;U] small plant with three, or rarely, four leaves on each stem: *He found a four-leaf clover.*

cold /kold/ *adj* low in temperature ♦ *n* **1** [U] low temperature **2** [C;U] illness of the nose and throat

come /kʌm/ *v* [I] **came** /kem/, **come 1** move towards the speaker; arrive **2** reach a particular point: *The water came up to my neck.* **3** have a particular position or order: *Monday comes after Saturday.* **4** be offered, produced, etc.: *Shoes come in different sizes.* | *Milk comes from cows.*

come out *phr v* [I] **1** appear **2** become known **3** (of color, etc.) be removed **4** end up: *How did everything come out?* **5** (of a photograph) be successful

com·mon /ˈkɑmən/ *adj* **1** ordinary; usual: *common salt* | *the common cold* **2** shared in a group: *common knowledge*

common sense *n* [U] practical good sense gained from experience

com·pass /ˈkʌmpəs/ *n* instrument for showing direction, with a needle that always points to the north

com·plain /kəmˈplen/ *v* [I/T] say that one is unhappy: *to complain that the room is too hot*

com·plaint /kəmˈplent/ *n* [C;U] (statement of) complaining

con·cert /ˈkɑnsərt/ *n* **1** musical performance **2** **in concert** playing at a concert

con·fuse /kənˈfyuz/ *v* [T] **1** cause to be mixed up in the mind: *I'm confused.* **2** be unable to tell the difference between: *to confuse Jack and/with Paul* **3** make less clear: *confusing the issue* ~**fusing** *adj*

~**fusion** /-ˈfyuʒən/ *n* [U]

con·sid·er /kənˈsɪdər/ *v* **1** *v* [I/T +v-ing] think about **2** *v* [T] take into account; remember: *you have to consider your wife*

consist in /kənˈsɪst -/ *phr v* [T] *fml* have as a base; depend on

consist of *phr v* [T] be made up of

con·tact /ˈkɑntækt/ *n* [U] meeting; relationship ♦ *v* [T] reach by telephone, etc.

con·test /ˈkɑntest/ *n* [C] struggle; competition

con·trol /kənˈtrol/ *v* [T] **controlled 1** direct; have power over **2** hold back ♦ *n* **1** [U] power to control **2** [C;U] means of controlling **3** **out of control** (in)to a state of not being controlled

cook·ie /ˈkʊki/ *n* small sweet cake

cool /kul/ *adj* **1** a little cold **2** calm; unexcited ♦ *v* [I/T] make or become cool

cord·less /ˈkɔrdləs/ *adj* needing no electric wire to work, using batteries

could /kəd; *strong* kʊd/ *v aux* **1** (describes **can** in the past): *He could read when he was four.* **2** (used to describe what someone has said): *She asked if she could smoke.* **3** (used to show what is possible): *I think the accident could have been prevented.* **4** (used to make a request): *Could you help me?*

cov·er¹ /ˈkʌvər/ *v* [T] **1** spread something over; hide in this way: *cover the body with a sheet* **2** lie on the surface of; spread over (something): *furniture covered in dust*

cover² *n* [C] anything that protects or hides by covering: *cushion covers* | (*fig.*) *The business is a cover for illegal activity.* ~**ing** *n* something that covers or hides

crack·er /ˈkrækər/ *n* unsweetened biscuit

crash /kræʃ/ *v* **1** *v* [I/T] fall or hit violently: *The car crashed into a tree.* **2** *v* [I] make a sudden loud noise **3** *v* [I] move violently and noisily: *The elephant crashed through the fence.* ♦ *n* **1** violent vehicle accident: *a car/plane crash* **2** sudden loud noise

crawl /krɔl/ *v* [I] move slowly, esp. with the body close to the ground: *crawling babies/traffic*

cra·zy /ˈkrezi/ *adj* **1** insane; foolish **2** wildly excited

cream /krim/ *n* [U] **1** thick liquid that rises to the top of milk **2** soft mixture like this: *face cream* ♦ *adj* yellow-white ♦ *v* [T] make into a soft mixture: *creamed potatoes*

cre·ate /kriˈet/ *v* [T] cause (something new) to exist; make

creep¹ /krip/ *v* [I] **crept** /krept/ **1** move slowly and quietly; crawl **2** (of a plant) grow along the ground or a surface

creep² *n* *infml* unpleasant person

crop spray·ing /ˈkrɑp ˌsprein/ *n, adj* scattering liquid chemicals over fields of plants from the air

cut off phr v [T] **1** cut a piece from **2** separate **3** disconnect

dai·ry /ˈdɛəri/ n place where milk, butter, cheese, etc. are produced or sold

dance /dæns/ n (music for) a set of movements performed to music ♦ v [I/T] do a dance **dancer** n

dan·ger·ous /ˈdeɪndʒərəs/ adj not safe

dare /dɛər/ v **1** v [I] be brave enough (to): *He didn't dare (to) ask.* **2** v [T] ask to do something with risk: *I dared her to jump.* ♦ n challenge: *She jumped on a dare.*

date v [I/T] spend time with another person socially or romantically ♦ n a social or romantic meeting **dated** adj old fashioned

dead /dɛd/ adj no longer alive

dead·ly /ˈdɛdli/ adj **1** likely to cause death **2** total: *deadly enemies* ♦ adv like death: *deadly pale*

deal /diːl/ n **a great deal of** a very large amount of

de·cide /dɪˈsaɪd/ v [I/T + to-v] make a choice or judgment (about)

decide on phr v [T] choose (one thing instead of another)

de·lay /dɪˈleɪ/ v **1** v [T +v-ing] make later **2** v [I] act slowly ♦ n **1** [U] delaying **2** [C] example or time of being delayed

de·li·cious /dɪˈlɪʃəs/ adj (esp. of taste or smell) pleasing ~**ly** adv

de·man·ding /dɪˈmændɪŋ/ adj needing a lot of attention or effort

de·pres·sion /dɪˈprɛʃən/ n **1** low levels of business activity **2** sadness; low emotional state

de·serve /dɪˈzɜrv/ v [T +to-v] be worthy of: *She deserved to win.*

de·vel·op /dɪˈvɛləp/ v **1** v [I/T] (cause to) grow or become more advanced **2** v [T] begin to have: *develop measles* ~**ment** n [C;U]

de·vice /dɪˈvaɪs/ n instrument or tool

di·a·ry /ˈdaɪəri/ n (book for) a daily record of events in one's life ~**rist** n writer of a diary

die /daɪ/ v [I] **died**, pres. p. **dying** /ˈdaɪɪŋ/ stop living; become dead

dif·fe·rent /ˈdɪfərənt/ adj **1** unlike **2** separate *They go to different schools.* **3** various: *It comes in different colours.* **4** unusual

dif·fi·cult /ˈdɪfɪkʌlt/ adj **1** hard to do, understand, etc. **2** (of people) not easily pleased

dif·fi·cul·ty /ˈdɪfɪkʌlti/ n **1** [U] being difficult; trouble **2** [C] something difficult; problem

dis·ad·van·tage /ˌdɪsədˈvæntɪdʒ/ n [C;U] unfavorable condition

dis·ap·pear /ˌdɪsəˈpɪr/ v [I] **1** go out of sight **2** cease to exist ~**ance** n [C;U]

dis·ap·point /ˌdɪsəˈpɔɪnt/ v [T] fail to fulfil hopes ~**ed** adj sad at not seeing hopes fulfilled ~**ing** adj ~**ingly** adv ~**ment** n **1** [U] being disappointed **2** [C] something disappointing

di·sas·ter /dɪˈzæstər/ n [C;U] sudden serious misfortune ~**trous** adj ~**trously** adv

dis·cour·age /dɪˈskɜrɪdʒ/ v [T] **1** take away hope from **2** persuade not to do something ~**ing** adj

dis·cuss /dɪˈskʌs/ v [T] talk about

dis·gust /dɪˈskʌst/ n [U] dislike caused esp. by a bad smell or taste or bad behavior ♦ v [T] cause disgust in ~**ing** adj ~**ingly** adv

dis·or·der /dɪsˈɔrdər/ n [U] confusion ♦ v [T] put into disorder ~**ly** adj

dis·turb /dɪˈstɜrb/ v [T] **1** interrupt **2** worry: *disturbing news*

dive /daɪv/ v [I] **dived** or **dove** /doʊv/ **1** jump head first into water **2** go under water **3** (of a plane or bird) go down steeply and swiftly ♦ n act of diving **diver** n person who dives, or works on the sea bottom

di·vorce /dəˈvɔrs/ n **1** [C;U] legal ending of a marriage **2** [C] separation ♦ v **1** vt/i end a marriage by law **2** v [T] separate completely **divorcée**, fem. **divorcé** masc. /dəˌvɔrˈseɪ/ n [C] divorced person

get divorced (of two people) to divorce

do¹ /də; strong duː/ v aux **did** /dɪd/, **done** /dʌn/ **1** (used with another verb): *Do you like it? | He doesn't know.* **2** (used instead of another verb): *He walks faster than I do. | She likes it, and so do I. | She sings, doesn't she?*

do² /duː/ v [T] **1** perform (an action); work at or produce: *do a chore/ one's homework/the cooking/ business/ one's best/one's duty | do* (= study) *Science at school* **2** **How do you do?** (used when one is introduced to someone) **3** **What do you do (for a living)?** What is your work?

dread /drɛd/ v [T +v-ing] fear greatly ♦ n [S;U] great fear

dried /draɪd/ adj (preserved by) having the liquid taken out

drive /draɪv/ v **drove** /droʊv/, **driven** /ˈdrɪvən/ **1** v [I/T] guide (a wheeled vehicle) **2** v [T] take (someone) in a vehicle **3** v [T] force (animals, etc.) to go **4** v [T] be the power for **5** v [T] send by hitting **6** v [T] force (someone) into a bad state: *The pain's driving me crazy.* **driver** n person who drives vehicles or animals

dy·na·mite /ˈdaɪnəˌmaɪt/ n [U] powerful explosive ♦ v [T] blow up with dynamite

eat /iːt/ v **ate** /eɪt/, **eaten** /ˈiːtn/ v [I/T] take in (food) through the mouth

e·lec·tric /ɪˈlɛktrɪk/ adj worked by or producing electricity: *an electric razor*

e·lec·tri·cian /ɪˌlɛkˈtrɪʃən/ n person who fits and repairs electrical equipment

e·lec·tri·ci·ty /ɪˌlɛkˈtrɪsəti/ n [U] power supply, carried usu. by wires, for heating, lighting, etc.

else /ɛls/ adv **1** more; as well: *What else can I say?* **2** apart from (what is mentioned): *He's here. Everyone else has gone home.* **3** otherwise: *You must pay or else go to prison.*

em·ploy·ee /ɪmˈplɔɪ-i, ˌɛmplɔɪˈi, ɪm-/ n employed person

emp·ty /ˈɛmpti/ adj **1** containing nothing **2** insincere: *empty promises* ♦ n [usu. pl.] empty container ♦ v [I/T] make or become empty ~**tiness** n [U]

en·joy /ɪnˈdʒɔɪ/ v [T +v-ing] **1** get pleasure from **2 enjoy oneself** be happy ~**able** adj pleasant ~**ably** adv ~**ment** n [C;U]

e·nough /ɪˈnʌf/ det, pron, adv as much or as many as is needed: *enough food/chairs | not big enough*

en·ter /ˈɛntər/ v [I/T] come or go in or into

en·trance /ˈɛntrəns/ n [C] door, etc., by which one enters

e·ven /ˈivən/ adv **1** (shows that something is unexpected and surprising): *John's a very good swimmer, but even he doesn't swim in the river.* **2** (makes comparisons stronger): *It's even colder than yesterday.*

ev·er /ˈɛvər/ adv at any time: *Does it ever snow?*

ex·am /ɪɡˈzæm/ n [C] **1** medical examination **2** test; school examination

ex·am·ine /ɪɡˈzæmɪn/ v [T] **1** look carefully at: *Has the doctor examined you yet?* **2** ask questions, to find out something or to test knowledge ~**iner** n ~**ination** n

ex·cite /ɪkˈsaɪt/ v [T] **1** cause to have strong (pleasant) feelings **2** fml cause (feelings): *excite interest* **exciting** adj **excited** adj

ex·ec·u·tive /ɪɡˈzɛkyətɪv/ adj concerned with managing, or carrying out decisions ♦ n person in an executive position in business

ex·haust /ɪɡˈzɔst/ v [T] **1** tire out **2** use up completely ~**ing** adj

ex·hib·it /ɪɡˈzɪbɪt/ v [T] show publicly for sale, etc. ♦ n something shown in a museum, etc. ~**or** n person showing exhibits

ex·pen·sive /ɪkˈspɛnsɪv/ adj costing a lot ~**ly** adv

ex·pe·ri·ence /ɪkˈspɪriəns/ n **1** [U] knowledge gained by practice ~**enced** adj having experience **2** [C] something that happens to one: *a fascinating experience* ♦ v [T] suffer or learn by experience: *to experience defeat*

ex·pla·na·tion /ˌɛkspləˈneɪʃən/ n **1** act of explaining **2** [C] something that explains

eye /aɪ/ n body part used to see with

fail /feɪl/ v **1** v [I/T +to-v] be unsuccessful or unable **2** v [I] not do what is wanted: *The crops/business failed.* **3** v [T] judge to be unsuccessful in a test **4** v [T] disappoint or leave (someone) at a bad time: *My courage failed me.*

faith·ful /ˈfeɪθfəl/ adj **1** loyal **2** true to the facts: *a faithful copy* ~**ly** adv

fall /fɔl/ v [I] **fell** /fɛl/, **fallen** /ˈfɔlən/ **1** come or go down freely: *She fell into the lake. | The house fell down.* **2** become: *fall asleep/in love* ♦ n [C] **1** long drop **2** autumn

fan /fæn/ n enthusiastic supporter

fare /fɛər/ n [C] money charged for a journey

farm·er /ˈfɑrmər/ n [C] person who grows large quantities of food for sale or trade

fas·ci·nate /ˈfæsəˌneɪt/ v [T] attract and interest strongly ~**nated** adj ~**nating** adj ~**nation** /ˌfæsəˈneɪʃən/ n [S;U]

fash·ion ed·i·tor /ˈfæʃən ˌɛdɪtər/ n person in charge of writing about clothes in a magazine/newspaper

feed /fiːd/ v **fed** /fɛd/ **1** v [T] give food to **2** v [I] (esp. of animals) eat **3** v [T] supply; provide

fight /faɪt/ v [I/T] **1** use violence (against); struggle **2** argue ♦ n [C] battle; struggle; argument

fight against phr v [T] do battle with (esp. in war)

fill out phr v [T] put in (what is necessary): *fill out a form*

film /fɪlm/ n **1** [U] thin material used in photography **2** [C] cinema picture; movie

fi·nal /ˈfaɪnl/ adj **1** last **2** (of a decision, etc.) that cannot be changed ~**ly** adv

find /faɪnd/ v [T] **found** /faʊnd/ **1** get (something lost or not known) by searching **2** learn by chance or effort: *find (out) where he lives*

fire¹ /faɪər/ n **1** [U] condition of burning: *afraid of fire* **2** [C] something burning, on purpose or by accident: *light a fire*

fire² v [T] dismiss from a job

first /fɜrst/ determiner, adv before any others: *my first visit* ♦ n, pron [S] person or thing before others: *the first to arrive*

first aid n [U] treatment given by an ordinary person to someone hurt in an accident, etc.

fish /fɪʃ/ n **fish 1** [C] creature that has cold blood and lives in water **2** [U] its flesh as food ♦ v [I] try to catch fish

flare /flɛər/ n bright light used as a signal

flash·light /ˈflæʃlaɪt/ n small electric light carried in the hand

flight attendant /ˈflaɪt əˌtɛndənt/ n person on an aircraft who serves passengers

float /floʊt/ v [I/T] (cause to) stay on the surface of liquid or be held up in air

fly /flaɪ/ v **1** v [I] move through the air as a bird or aircraft does **2** v [T] control (an aircraft)

fol·low /ˈfɑloʊ/ v **1** v [I/T] come or go after **2** v [T] go along: *follow the river* **3** v [T] act according to: *follow instructions*

foot /fʊt/ n **feet** /fiːt/ **1** [C] end part of the leg **2** [S] bottom: *foot of the stairs* **3** [C] twelve inches

for·eign /ˈfɔrɪn/ adj from another country ~**er** n foreign person

for·mal /ˈfɔrməl/ adj **1** suitable for official or polite occasions **2** stiff in manner and behavior **~ly** *adv*

fre·quent /ˈfrikwənt/ *adj* happening often **~ly** *adv*

fresh /frɛʃ/ *adj* **1** recently made, found, etc.: *fresh flowers* **2** (of food) not frozen or canned **3** (of water) not salt **~ly** *adv* **~ness** *n*

friend /frɛnd/ *n* person one likes but who is not related **~ly** *adj* **1** acting as a friend **2** not causing unpleasant feelings: *a friendly game*

fright·en /ˈfraɪtn/ *v* [T] fill with fear **~ed** *adj* **~ing** *adj* **~ingly** *adv*

fruit /frut/ *n* [C;U] part of a plant containing the seed, often eatable

gas can·is·ter /ˈgæs ˌkænɪstər/ *n* container for holding a substance like air, used for cooking, heating, etc.

get /gɛt/ *v* **got** /gɑt/, **gotten** /ˈgɑtn/ *or* **got** *pres. p.* **getting** **1** *v* [T] receive; obtain: *get a letter* | *get permission* **2** *v* [T] collect; bring **3** *v* [T] catch (an illness) **4** *v* [I/T] (cause to) go or arrive: *get home* **5** [+adj] become: *get sick/married* **6** *v* [T] prepare (a meal) **7** **get (something) done**: cause something to be done: *I must get these shoes mended.*

get back *phr v* [I] **1** return **2** tell a person at a later time: *I can't tell you now, but I'll get back to you tomorrow.*

get in *phr v* **1** *v* [I] arrive: *The plane got in late.* **2** *v* [T] enter (a car or truck)

get off *phr v* **1** *v* [I] leave; start **2** *v* [T] leave (a large or open vehicle)

get on *phr v* [I] **1** approach old age **2** be on friendly terms **3** proceed; continue: *get on with the game* **4** *v* [T] enter (a large or open vehicle): bus, train, plane, bicycle, boat)

get out *phr v* **1** *v* [I/T] (cause to) escape **2** *v* [T] leave (a car or truck)

get up *phr v* [I] rise from bed

ghost /gost/ *n* (spirit of) a dead person who appears again

gi·gan·tic /dʒaɪˈgæntɪk/ *adj* very large

give /gɪv/ *v* **gave** /gev/, **given** /ˈgɪvən/ **1** *v* [T] cause or allow someone to have: *give him a present/a job* **2** *v* [T] pay in exchange: *I'll give $3000 for the car.* **3** *v* [I] supply money: *give generously to charity* **4** *v* [T] perform (an action): *give an order*

give back *phr v* [T] return (something) to the owner

give in *phr v* [I] give up

give off *phr v* [T] send out (a smell)

give out *phr v* [T] distribute

give up *phr v* **1** *v* [I/T] stop: *give up smoking* **2** *v* [T] regard as lost or hopeless

glue /glu/ *n* [U] sticky substance for joining things

go /go/ *v* **went** /wɛnt/, **gone** /gɔn, gɑn/ **1** *v* [I] leave a place: *I have to go now.* **2** *v* [I] move; travel: *go by bus* | *go shopping* **3** *v* [I] lead; reach: *This road goes to the West Coast.* **4** become: *go crazy*

go back *phr v* [I] **1** return **2** stretch back in time

go out with *phr v* [T] date romantically

good /gʊd/ *adj* **better** /ˈbɛtər/, **best** /bɛst/ **1** satisfactory: *good food/ brakes* **2** pleasant: *good news* | *have a good time* **3** useful; suitable: *Milk is good for you.* **4** clever: *good at math* **5** well-behaved **6** morally right: *good deeds*

grab /græb/ *v* [I/T] **-bb-** seize suddenly and roughly

grain /gren/ *n* **1** [C] single seed of rice, wheat, etc. **2** [U] crops from food plants like these **3** small hard piece: *grains of sand*

great /gret/ *adj* **1** excellent and important: *great writers* **2** large: *great pleasure* | *a great many people* **3** to an extreme degree: *great friends* **5** very good: *a great film* **6** grand-: one more generation than grand-: *his great-grandfather* | *his great-granddaughter*

green thumb /grin ˈθʌm/ *n* [S] natural skill in making plants grow

Green·wich Village /ˌgrɛnɪtʃ ˈvɪlədʒ/ *n* area of New York City

grow /gro/ *v* **grew** /gru/, **grown** /gron/ **1** *v* [I] get bigger **2** *v* [I] (of plants) live and develop **3** *v* [T] cause (plants, etc.) to grow **4** *fml* become: *grow old*

guide /gaɪd/ *n* **1** person who shows the way **2** something that influences behavior **3** *also* **guide book** book describing a place **4** instruction book ♦ *v* [T] act as a guide to

gun /gʌn/ *n* weapon that fires bullets

gur·gle /ˈgɜrgəl/ *vi, n* (make) the sound of water flowing unevenly **gurgling** *adj*

hand in /hænd ˈɪn/ *phr v* [T] deliver

hand·some /ˈhænsəm/ *adj* of good appearance: *a handsome boy*

hang-glid·ing /ˈhæŋ ˌglaɪdɪŋ/ *n* [U] floating in the air attached to a large kite

har·bor /ˈhɑrbər/ *n* area of water where ships are safe

hate /het/ *v* [T + *to-v*, + *v-ing*] dislike very much ♦ *n* [C;U] strong dislike

haunt /hɔnt/ *v* **1** (of a spirit) appear in **2** visit regularly

have *v* [T] **1** possess: *She has two sisters.* **2** experience or enjoy: *to have a party/a vacation* **3** cause to be done: *You should have your hair cut.*

head·ache /ˈhɛdek/ *n* **1** pain in the head **2** problem

hear /hɪər/ *v* **heard** /hɜrd/ **1** *v* [I/T] receive (sounds) with the ears **2** *v* [T] be told or informed: *I hear they're married.*

heart /hɑrt/ *n* **1** [C] organ that pumps blood around the body **2** [C] center of a person's feelings: *a kind heart.* **3** [C] something shaped like a heart **4** [C] center: *heart of the city.*

heat¹ /hit/ *n* [U] **1** (degree of) hotness **2** hot weather: *I don't like the heat much.*

heat² *v* [I/T] make or become hot **~ed** *adj* excited and angry **~er** *n* machine for heating **~ing** *n* [U] system for keeping rooms warm

heav·y /ˈhɛvi/ *adj* **1** of great weight **2** of unusual amount: *heavy rain /traffic* | *a heavy smoker* (= someone who smokes a lot)

hel·lo /həˈlo/ *interj, n* **-los** (used in greeting and answering a telephone)

help /hɛlp/ *v* **1** *v* [I/T] make it possible for (someone) to do something; be useful (to) **2** **can't help** *v* [T+*v-ing*] avoid; prevent: *I can't help laughing.*

here /hɪər/ *adv* at, in, or to this place

high /haɪ/ *adj* **1** far above the ground: *a high mountain* | *20 feet high* **2** great: *high cost* **3** good: *high standards*

hike /haɪk/ *vi, n* (go for) a long country walk

hire /haɪər/ *v* [T] start employment; get the use or services of someone for payment: *hire a teacher*

his /hɪz/ *weak ɪz/ determiner* of him: *his shoes* ♦ *pron* of him; his one(s): *It's his.*

hold up /hold ˈʌp/ *phr v* [T] **1** delay **2** rob by force ♦ **holdup** /ˈholdʌp/ *n* [C] **1** delay **2** armed robbery

hom·i·cide /ˈhɑməˌsaɪd/ *n* [C;U] *fml* murder

hook /hʊk/ *n* curved piece of metal or plastic for catching, hanging, or fastening things ♦ *v* [T] catch, hang, or fasten with a hook **~ed** *adj* shaped like a hook

hor·ri·ble /ˈhɔrəbəl/ *adj* **1** causing horror **2** very unpleasant **~bly** *adv*

hor·ror /ˈhɔrər/ *n* [C;U] (something causing) great shock and fear

hot /hɑt/ *adj* **-tt-** **1** having a high temperature **2** having a burning taste: *hot pepper* **3** (of news) very recent **4** **hottest** newest; most fashionable

hour /aʊər/ *n* sixty minutes

house·hold /ˈhaʊshold/ *n* all the people living in a house

hug /hʌg/ *v* [T] **-gg-** hold tightly in one's arms **hug** *n*

huge /hyudʒ/ *adj* very big **~ly** *adv* very much

hum /hʌm/ *v* **-mm-** **1** *v* [I] buzz **2** *v* [I/T] sing with closed lips **3** *v* [I] be full of activity ♦ *n* [U]

hunt /hʌnt/ *v* [I/T] **1** chase (animals) for food or sport **2** search (for)

I *pron* (used for the person speaking, as the subject of a sentence)

i·ma·gine /ɪˈmædʒɪn/ *v* [T] **1** form (an idea) in the mind: *imagine a world without cars* **2** believe; suppose: *I imagine they've forgotten.* **~gin·able** *adj* that can be imagined **~ginative** *adj* good at imagining **~gination** /ɪˌmædʒəˈneʃən/ *n* **1** [C;U] ability to imagine **2** [U] something only imagined

in·cred·i·ble /ɪnˈkrɛdəbəl/ *adj* **1** unbelievable **2** *infml* wonderful **~bly** *adv*

in·spire /ɪnˈspaɪər/ *v* [T] **1** encourage to act **2** fill with a feeling: *inspire them with confidence*

in·stru·ment /ˈɪnstrəmənt/ *n* apparatus for playing music

in·tel·li·gent /ɪnˈtɛlədʒənt/ *adj* having the ability to learn and understand

in·tend /ɪnˈtɛnd/ *v* [T +*to-v*] have as one's purpose; mean

in·ter·est·ed /ˈɪntrəstɪd/ *adj* **1** willing to give attention **2** personally concerned **interesting** *adj* having a quality that makes people pay attention

in·ter·rupt /ˌɪntəˈrʌpt/ *v* [I/T] break the flow of (speech, etc.) **~ion** /-ˈrʌpʃən/ *n* [C;U]

in·ter·view /ˈɪntərˌvyu/ *n* meeting where a person is asked questions ♦ *v* [T] ask (someone) questions in an interview **~ee** *n* person who is being or is to be interviewed, esp. for a job **~er** *n* person who interviews

in·ves·ti·gate /ɪnˈvɛstəˌget/ *v* [I/T] inquire carefully (about): *investigate a crime* **~gator** *n* **~gative** *adj* **~gation** *n* [C;U]

in·vite /ɪnˈvaɪt/ *v* [T] **1** ask to come **2** ask politely for: *invite questions* **inviting** *adj*

i·ron¹ /ˈaɪərn/ *n* **1** [U] common hard metal used in making steel, etc. **2** [C] heavy object for making cloth smooth

iron² *v* [T] make smooth with an iron

ir·ri·tate /ˈɪrəˌtet/ *v* [T] **1** annoy **2** make sore **~ing** *adj* **~tation** /ˌɪrəˈteʃən/ *n* [C;U]

i·so·la·ted /ˈaɪsəˌletɪd/ *adj* **1** kept separate from others **2** alone; only: *an isolated case*

itch /ɪtʃ/ *v* [I] have the feeling of wanting to scratch the skin ♦ *n* itching feeling

its /ɪts/ *det* of it: *its ears*

it's /ɪts/ *short for:* **1** it is **2** it has

jeal·ous /ˈdʒɛləs/ *adj* **1** unhappy at not being liked as much as someone else: *jealous husband* **2** wanting what someone else has **3** wanting to keep what one has **~ly** *adv*

jew·el·ry /ˈdʒuəlri/ *n* [U] stones or other things, worn as decoration

job /dʒɑb/ *n* **1** [C] regular paid employment: *out of a job* (= unemployed) **2** [C] piece of work **3** [S] one's affair; duty: *It's not my job to interfere.*

jour·nal /ˈdʒɜrnl/ *n* diary **~ism** *n* [U] profession of writing for newspapers **~ist** *n* person whose profession is journalism

juice /dʒus/ *n* [C;U] liquid from fruit, vegetables, or meat **juicy** *adj* having a lot of juice

jump /dʒʌmp/ *v* **1** *v* [I] push suddenly off the ground: *The horse jumped over the fence.* **2** *v* [I] move suddenly: *The noise made me jump.* **3** *v* [I] rise sharply: *Oil prices have jumped.*

keep /kip/ *v* **kept** /kɛpt/ **1** *v* [T] continue to have **2** *v* [I/T] (cause to) continue being: *keep them warm* | *Keep off the grass!*

keep back *phr v* [T] not tell or give; withhold

keep off *phr v* [T] don't touch

keep on *phr v* [T +*v-ing*] continue **keep on good terms with** remain friendly with

keep on at *phr v* [T] ask repeatedly

keep out *phr v* [I/T] (cause to) stay away or not enter

keep up *phr v* [T] **1** continue doing **2** prevent from going to bed **3** prevent from falling: *my belt keeps my pants up*

key /ki/ *n* **1** shaped piece of metal for locking a door, etc. **2** a button pressed to produce a desired sound or effect: *A piano has black and white keys.* | *The keys on my typewriter are very quiet.*

kid·nap /'kɪdnæp/ *v* [T] –**pp**– take (someone) away by force, so as to demand money, etc. **~per** *n*

kit /kɪt/ *n* necessary clothes, tools, etc.: *a sailor's/carpenter's kit*

know /no/ *v* **knew** /nu/, **known** /non/ **1** *v* [I/T] have (information) in the mind **2** *v* [T] have learned **3** *v* [T] be familiar with: *Do you know Paris well?* **4** *v* [T] be able to recognize: *You'll know him by his red hair.*

lace /les/ *n* **1** [U] netlike decorative cloth **2** [C] cord for fastening shoes, etc.

lad·der /'lædər/ *n* bars joined to each other by steps, for climbing

land·ing /'lændɪŋ/ *n* **1** level space at the top of a set of stairs **2** arrival on land: *crash landing*

laugh /læf/ *v* [I] express amusement, happiness, etc., by breathing out strongly so that one makes sounds with the voice, usu. while smiling

law /lɔ/ *n* **1** [C] rule made by a government **2** [U] all these rules: *Stealing is against the law.*

learn /lɜrn/ *v* [I/T] **1** gain (knowledge or skill): *learn French* | *learn to swim* **2** fix in the memory: *learn a poem*

leave /liv/ *v* **left** /lɛft/ **1** *v* [I/T] go away (from) **2** *v* [T] allow to remain: *leave the door open* | *Is there any coffee left?* **3** *v* [T] fail to take or bring: *I've left my coat behind.*

lec·ture /'lɛktʃər/ *n* **1** speech given as a method of teaching **2** long solemn scolding or warning ◆ *v* [I/T] give a lecture (to)

lie[1] /laɪ/ *vi, n* **lied**, *pres. p.* **lying** (make) a false statement

lie[2] /laɪ/ [I] **lay** /le/, **lain** /len/, *pres. p.* **lying** /'laɪ-ɪŋ/ be or remain in a flat position on a surface

lie down *phr v* [I] put oneself in a lying position **lie down on the job** do work that is not good enough in quantity or quality **take something lying down** suffer something bad without complaining or trying to stop it

lift /lɪft/ *v* [T] **1** raise to a higher level **2** improve: *lift my spirits*

like /laɪk/ *v* [T + to-v, +v-ing] **1** regard with pleasure or fondness **2** be willing (to): *I don't like to ask.*

3 (with **would**) wish or choose (to have): *I'd like a boiled egg.* | *Would you like to read it?*

line up /laɪn ʌp/ *phr v* **1** [I/T] form into a row esp. to wait for something **2** *vt* arrange (an event)

lis·ten /'lɪsən/ *v* [I] give attention to in hearing

lit·tle /'lɪtl/ *n* [S] (with **a**) a small amount: *Stay a little longer.*

live /lɪv/ *v* [I] **1** be alive **2** remain alive: *The doctor says he'll live.* **3** have one's home: *live in Paris*

lone·ly /'lonli/ *adj* **1** alone and unhappy **2** (of places) without people

look /lʊk/ *v* [I] **1** use the eyes to see something **2** seem; appear: *You look tired.*

look at *phr v* [T] to watch or observe

look for *phr v* [T] try to find

look forward to *phr v* [T] expect to enjoy

look through *phr v* [T] search

look up *phr v* **1** *v* [I] improve **2** *v* [T] find (information) in a book

lot·te·ry /'lɑtəri/ *n* system of giving prizes to people who bought numbered tickets, chosen by chance

love /'lʌv/ *n* great fondness for someone or something ◆ *v* [T] show great fondness for someone or something **love at first sight** love at the first time of seeing or meeting

lov·er /'lʌvər/ *n* **1** person who has a sexual relationship with another **2** person who is fond of the stated thing: *art lovers*

love·sick /'lʌvˌsɪk/ *adj* sad because of unreturned love

lov·ing /'lʌvɪŋ/ *adj* showing great fondness for someone

low·er[1] /'loər/ *adj* at or nearer the bottom: *the lower leg*

lower[2] *v* [T] make less high **lower oneself** bring oneself down in people's opinion

luck /lʌk/ *n* [U] **1** what happens to someone by chance **2** success: *wish them luck*

ma·chine /mə'ʃin/ *n* instrument or apparatus that uses power to work

mag·ic /'mædʒɪk/ *n* **1** use of strange unseen forces, or of tricks, to produce effects **2** special wonderful quality: *the magic of the theater* ◆ *adj* caused by or used in magic: *a magic trick/ring* **~al** *adj* strange and wonderful **~ly** /-kli/ *adv*

ma·gi·cian /mə'dʒɪʃən/ *n* person who practices or entertains with magic

mail /mel/ *n* [U] **1** the official system for carrying letters, parcels, etc. **2** letters, etc., that one sends or receives ◆ *v* [T] send through this system

ma·jor /'medʒər/ *adj* of great importance or seriousness: *a major problem* | *major surgery*

make /mek/ *v* [T] **made** /med/ **1** produce: *make a cake/a noise/a decision* **2** cause to be: *It made me*

happy. **3** earn (money) **4** tidy (a bed that has been slept in) **maker** *n* person who makes something

mal·ad·just·ed /ˌmæləd'ʒʌstɪd/ *adj* not fitting in well with other people or with life generally

man·a·ger /'mænɪdʒər/ *n* person who runs a business, hotel, sports team, etc.

man·ta ray /'mæntə ˌre/ *n* type of large fish having a wide, flat body and winglike fins

map /mæp/ *n* representation of (part of) the Earth's surface as if seen from above

mar·riage /'mærɪdʒ/ *n* [C;U] **1** ceremony to marry people **2** state of being husband and wife

mar·ry /'mæri/ *v* [I/T] take (as) a husband or wife: *She married a soldier.* **married** *adj* **1** having a husband or wife: *a married man* **married to** having as a husband or wife: *He's married to a doctor.*

match[1] /mætʃ/ *n* sports or other competition between two people or sides; game

match[2] *n* short thin stick that burns when its end is rubbed against a rough surface

math /mæθ/ *n* science of numbers; mathematics, arithmetic

math·e·ma·ti·cian /ˌmæθəmə'tɪʃən/ *n* person skilled in math

meal /mil/ *n* (food eaten at) an occasion for eating

mea·sure /'mɛʒər/ *v* [T] **1** find or show the size, amount, degree, etc. of: *Measure the (height of the) cupboard first.* **2** be of the stated size: *The river measured 200 yards from side to side.* **~surable** *adj* **~surably** *adv*

meat /mit/ *n* [U] flesh of animals (not fish) for eating

mem·ber /'mɛmbər/ *n* someone who belongs to a club, group, etc. **~ship** *n* [C;U]

might /maɪt/ *v aux* (used for expressing slight possibility): *He might come, but it's unlikely.*

mil·lion /'mɪlyən/ *det, n, pron* [C] 1,000,000; a thousand thousands

miss /mɪs/ *v* **1** *v* [I/T +v-ing] fail to hit, catch, meet, see, hear, etc.: *He shot at me, but missed.* | *I missed the train.* | *She narrowly missed being killed.* **2** *v* [T] feel unhappy at the absence or loss of

mis·take /mɪ'stek/ *v* [T] **–took** /mɪ'stʊk/, **–taken** /mɪ'stekən/ have a wrong idea about: *He mistook my meaning.* ◆ *n* [C;U] something done through carelessness, lack of knowledge or skill, etc.: *I made a terrible mistake.* | *I did it by mistake.*

month /mʌnθ/ *n* twelfth part of a year **~ly** *adj*

mo·ray eel /'mɔre ˌil/ *n* type of brightly colored eel with sharp teeth

move /muv/ *v* [I/T] (cause to) change place or position: *Sit still and don't move!* | *move up/down*

mov·ie /'muvi/ *n* cinema film **movies**

n [the+P] cinema: *What's on at the movies?* | *Let's go to the movies.*

mur·der /'mɜrdər/ *n* [C;U] crime of killing someone intentionally ◆ *v* [T] kill illegally and intentionally

mu·se·um /myu'ziəm/ *n* building where objects of historical, scientific, or artistic interest are kept and shown

mu·sic /'myuzɪk/ *n* [U] **1** sounds arranged in patterns, usu. with tunes **2** art of making music **3** printed representation of music **~ian** /myu'zɪʃən/ *n*

mys·te·ry /'mɪstəri/ *n* **1** [C] something which cannot be explained or understood **2** [U] strange secret quality **~rious** /mɪ'stɪəriəs/ *adj* unexplainable: *his mysterious disappearance*

nap /næp/ *n* short sleep ◆ *v* [I] –**pp**– have a nap

nat·u·ral /'nætʃərəl/ *adj* existing or happening ordinarily in the world, esp. not made by people: *death from natural causes*

near /nɪər/ *adj* at a short distance; close ◆ *adv, prep* not far (from) **~ly** *adv*

neat /nit/ *adj* **1** tidy **2** simple and effective: *a neat trick* **3** pleasing: *a really neat new car*

ne·ces·si·ty /nə'sɛsəti/ *n* **1** [S;U] condition of being necessary; need **2** [C] something necessary, esp. for life

neck·lace /'nɛk-lɪs/ *n* decorative chain or string of jewels, worn around the neck

need[1] /nid/ *n* **1** [S;U] condition in which something necessary or desirable is missing: *a need for better medical services* **2** [S;U] necessary duty: *There's no need for you to come.* **~less** *adj* **1** unnecessary **2** needless to say of course **~lessly** *adv* **~y** *adj* poor

need[2] *v* [T] have a need for; want: *To survive, plants need water.*

need[3] *v* [T +to-v] have to; must: *Do you think I need to go to the meeting?*

neigh·bor /'nebər/ *n* someone who lives next door, or near

next /nɛkst/ *adj* **1** with nothing before or between; nearest: *the house next to mine* **2** the one following or after: *I'm coming next week.* ◆ *adv* just afterwards: *Next, add the onions.*

nice /naɪs/ *adj* good; pleasant: *have a nice day* **~ly** *adv* **~ness** *n* [U]

no /no/ *adv* **1** (used for refusing or disagreeing): *'Do you like it?' 'No!'* **2** not any: *He felt no better.* ◆ *determiner* **1** not a; not any: *She felt no fear.* **2** (shows what is not allowed): *No smoking* (on a sign)

noise /nɔɪz/ *n* [C;U] sound, esp. loud and unpleasant **noisy** *adj* making a lot of noise **noisily** *adv* **noisiness** *n* [U]

nurse /nɜrs/ *n* person who takes care of sick, hurt, or old people, esp. in a hospital ◆ *v* [T] take care of as or like a nurse

of·fice /ˈɔfɪs/ n 1 [C] room or building where written work is done 2 [C] place where a particular service is provided: *a ticket office* 3 [C;U] important job or position of power: *the office of president*

oil /ɔɪl/ n [U] thick fatty liquid that burns easily, esp. petroleum ♦ v [T] put oil on or into **~y** adj

on·ly[1] /ˈonli/ adj 1 with no others in the same group: *my only friend* | *an only child* (= with no brothers or sisters) 2 best: *She's the only person for this job.*

only[2] adv 1 and no one or nothing else: *There were only five left.* 2 **if only** (expresses a strong wish): *If only she were here!*

only[3] conj except that; but: *She wants to go, only she doesn't have enough money.*

op·e·rate /ˈɒpəret/ v 1 v [I/T] (cause to) work: *learning to operate the controls* 2 v [I] do business: *We operate throughout Europe.* 3 v [I] cut the body to cure or remove diseased parts, usu. in a hospital

op·po·nent /əˈponənt/ n 1 person who takes the opposite side

or·gan·i·za·tion /ˌɔrgənəˈzeʃən/ n group of people with a special purpose, such as a business or club

or·gan·ize /ˈɔrgənaɪz/ v [T] 1 arrange into a good system: *a well-organized office* 2 make necessary arrangements for: *to organize a party* **~ed** adj

our /aʊər, ar/ det of us: *our house*

out·fit /ˈaʊtˌfɪt/ n set of things esp. clothes for a particular purpose

own[1] /on/ det, pron belonging to the stated person and no one else: *At last I had my own room/a room of my own.*

own[2] v [T] possess, esp. by legal right **~er** n **~ership** n [U]

ox·y·gen /ˈɒksədʒən/ n gas present in the air, necessary for life

pack /pæk/ v 1 v [I/T] put (things) into cases, boxes, etc., for taking somewhere or storing 2 v [I/T] fit or push into a space

pair /peər/ n 1 two of the same kind, but usu. matching: *a pair of gloves* 2 something made of two similar parts: *a pair of scissors* 3 two people closely connected

pair off phr v [I/T] form into one or more pairs: *Jane and David paired off at the party.*

par·a·ple·gic /ˌpærəˈplidʒɪk/ adj, n (of or being) a person suffering from loss of feeling in and control of the lower part of the body

par·tic·i·pate /parˈtɪsəpet/ v [I] take part (in an activity)

par·tic·u·lar·ly /pərˈtɪkyələrli/ adv especially

part-time /part ˈtaɪm/ adj, adv not all the (regular) time esp. of working

pa·tient /ˈpeʃənt/ adj having the ability to wait calmly, to control oneself when angered, or to accept unpleasant things without complaining

pawn·shop /ˈpɔnʃɑp/ n shop where one can borrow money after giving something valuable which can be reclaimed by repaying the money

pear /peər/ n sweet, juicy fruit, narrow at the stem end and wide at the other

pe·di·at·rics /ˌpidiˈætrɪks/ n [S] branch of medicine concerned with children **~rician** /ˌpidiəˈtrɪʃən/ n children's doctor

per·fect /ˈpərfɪkt/ adj 1 of the very best possible kind, standard, etc. 2 as good or suitable as possible: *Your English is almost perfect.* **~ly** adv

per·form /pərˈfɔrm/ v 1 v [T] do (a piece of work, ceremony, etc.): *to perform an operation* 2 v [I/T] act or show (a play, piece of music, etc.), esp. in public 3 v [I] work or carry out an activity (in the stated way): *a car that performs well in the mountains* **~ance** n [C] (public) show of music, a play, etc. **~er** n actor, musician, etc.

pet /pet/ n animal kept for company

phar·ma·cist /ˈfɑrməsɪst/ n person who makes medicines

phar·ma·cy /ˈfɑrməsi/ n 1 [C] drugstore; place where medicines are given out 2 [U] making or giving out of medicines

pho·to·graph /ˈfotəgræf/ n picture taken with a camera and film **~er** /fəˈtɑgrəfər/ n person who takes photographs for pleasure or as a business **~y** /fəˈtɑgrəfi/ n art or business of making photographs **~ic** /fotəˈgræfɪk/ adj

phrase /frez/ n 1 group of words without a finite verb 2 short (suitable) expression

pick up phr v [T] 1 take hold of and lift up 2 gather together: *Pick up your toys.*

pick·le /ˈpɪkəl/ n [C;U] cucumber preserved in vinegar or salt water ♦ **pickled** adj preserved in vinegar or salt water

piece /pis/ n 1 separate part or bit: *pieces of broken glass* 2 single object that is an example of its kind or class: *a piece of paper/music/* (fig.) *advice*

pil·low /ˈpɪlo/ n filled cloth bag for supporting the head in bed

pipe /paɪp/ n 1 tube carrying liquid or gas 2 small tube with a bowl-like container, for smoking tobacco

plane /plen/ n airplane; aircraft

play·ground /ˈplegraʊnd/ n piece of ground for children to play on

pleas·ant /ˈplɛzənt/ adj pleasing; nice **~ly** adv

plow /plaʊ/ n farming tool for breaking up earth and turning it over ♦ v [I/T] break up and turn over (earth) with a plow

plumb·er /ˈplʌmər/ n person who fits and repairs water pipes

pol·i·ti·cian /ˌpɑləˈtɪʃən/ n person whose business is politics

pol·i·tics /ˈpɑlətɪks/ n [U] the activity of winning and using government power, in competition with other parties: *active in local politics*

pop·u·lar /ˈpɑpyələr/ adj 1 liked by many people: *a popular restaurant* 2 common; widespread: *a popular name* 3 of the general public: **~ly** adv **~ity** /ˌpɑpyəˈlærəti/ n [U]

post·mark /ˈpostmɑrk/ n official mark on a letter, etc., showing where and when it was posted ♦ vt

pound /paʊnd/ v 1 v [I/T] strike repeatedly and heavily 2 v [I] move with quick heavy steps **pounding** adj (fig.) *a pounding headache*

pow·er·ful /ˈpaʊərfəl/ adj 1 full of force: *a powerful engine* 2 great in degree: *a powerful smell* 3 having much control or influence

pre·dict /prɪˈdɪkt/ v [T] say in advance (what will happen) **~able** adj 1 that can be predicted 2 not doing anything unexpected **~ably** adv **~ion** /prɪˈdɪkʃən/ n [C;U] predicting or something predicted

pre·fix /ˈpriˌfɪks/ n wordlike part added at the beginning of a word to change its meaning (as in *untie*)

pre·his·tor·ic /ˌprihɪˈstɔrɪk/ adj before recorded history **~ally** /-kli/ adv

pre·vent /prɪˈvent/ v [T] stop (something) happening or (someone) doing something **~ion** /prɪˈvenʃən/ n

pre·view /ˈprivyu/ n private showing or short description of film, show, etc., before it is publicly seen ♦ v [T] give a preview of

pri·vate /ˈpraɪvət/ adj 1 not (to be) shared with others; secret 2 just for one person or a small group, not everyone 3 not connected with or paid for by government: *private school* 4 quiet; without lots of people **~ly** adv

private de·tec·tive /- dəˈtɛktɪv/ n person, not a policeman, hired to find out information about people

prize /praɪz/ n something you are given for winning, doing well, etc.

pro·duce /prəˈdus/ v [T] 1 bring into existence; give: *These trees produce rubber.* 2 make (goods for sale)

proof /pruf/ n 1 [C;U] way of showing that something is true 2 [C] a test or trial

pro·tect /prəˈtɛkt/ v [T] keep safe **~ion** n 1 [U] act of protecting or state of being protected 2 [C] something that protects

psy·chi·a·try /saɪˈkaɪətri/ n [U] study and treatment of diseases of the mind **~trist** n **~tric** /ˌsaɪkiˈætrɪk/ adj

psy·chic /ˈsaɪkɪk/ adj 1 having strange powers, such as the ability to see into the future 2 of the mind 3 connected with the spirits of the dead **~ally** /-li/ adv

psy·chol·o·gy /saɪˈkɑlədʒi/ n [U] study of how the mind works **~gist** n

pump·kin /ˈpʌmpkɪn/ n [C;U] extremely large round orange vegetable

put away phr v [T] remove to its usual storing place

put in phr v [T] do (work) or spend (time) on work

put off phr v [T] 1 delay 2 discourage 3 cause to dislike

put out phr v [T] 1 cause to stop burning 2 trouble or annoy

put up with phr v [T] suffer without complaining

qui·et /ˈkwaɪət/ adj 1 with little noise 2 calm; untroubled: *a quiet life* ♦ n [U] 1 quietness 2 **keep something quiet** keep something a secret ♦ v [I/T] make or become quiet **~ly** adv **~ness** n [U]

raft /ræft/ n flat, usu. wooden floating structure, used esp. as a boat

rain·coat /ˈrenkot/ n a light coat worn to keep dry when it rains

raise /rez/ v [T] 1 lift 2 make higher in amount, size, etc. 3 produce and look after (children, animals, or crops) ♦ n wage increase

rare /reər/ adj uncommon

real·ly /ˈrili/ adv 1 in fact; truly 2 very

rea·so·na·ble /ˈrizənəbəl/ adj 1 showing fairness or good sense 2 not expensive

re·duce /rɪˈdus/ v [T] 1 make less 2 (of a person) lose weight on purpose

re·gret /rɪˈgret/ v [T +v-ing] –tt– be sorry about: *I've never regretted my decision to leave.* **~table** adj that one should regret **~tably** adv

reg·u·lar /ˈregyələr/ adj 1 usual or customary 2 not varying: *a regular pulse* | *a regular customer* 3 following the standard pattern: *regular verbs* **~ly** adv at regular times

re·lax /rɪˈlæks/ v [I/T] make or become less active, worried, stiff, tight, or severe **~ation** /ˌrilækˈseʃən/ n 1 [C;U] (something done for) rest and amusement 2 [U] act of making or becoming less severe **relaxed** adj **relaxing** adj

re·li·a·ble /rɪˈlaɪəbəl/ adj that may be trusted **~ably** adv **~ability** /rɪˌlaɪəˈbɪləti/ n [U]

re·mar·ka·ble /rɪˈmɑrkəbəl/ adj unusual or noticeable **~bly** adv

re·mem·ber /rɪˈmembər/ v 1 v [T +v-ing] call back into the mind 2 v [I/T + to-v] take care not to forget

re·pair·man /rɪˈpeərmæn/ n man who repairs things as a business

re·pair /rɪˈpeər/ v [I/T] fix; make something like new ♦ **~s** n [P] work done to make something like new

re·pel /rɪˈpel/ v –ll– 1 drive away (as if) by force 2 cause feelings of extreme dislike in

re·place /rɪˈples/ v [T] 1 put back in the right place 2 take the place of

re·port[1] /rɪˈpɔrt/ n [C] account of events, business affairs, etc.

report[2] v [I/T] provide information (about); give an account of, esp. for a newspaper or radio or television **~er** n person who reports news

re·pro·duce /ˌriprəˈdus/ v [I/T] 1 produce the young of (oneself or one's kind) 2 produce a copy (of)

res·cue /ˈreskyu/ v save or set free

from harm or danger **rescue** n ~**cuer** n

re·search /rɪˈsɜrtʃ/ n [C;U] advanced and detailed study, to find out (new) facts ♦ v [I/T] do research (on or for) ~**er** n

re·spect·ful /rɪˈspɛktfəl/ adj feeling or showing great admiration and honor

re·sult /rɪˈzʌlt/ n [C;U] what happens because of an action or event

re·tired /rɪˈtaɪərd/ adj having stopped working

ride¹ /raɪd/ v **rode** /rod/, **ridden** /ˈrɪdn/ **1** v [I/T] travel along on (a horse, etc., a bicycle, or a motorcycle) **2** vi travel on a bus

ride² n journey on an animal, in a vehicle, etc.

right¹ /raɪt/ adj **1 a** on the side of the body away from the heart **b** in the direction of one's right side **2** just; proper; morally good

right² n **1** [U] right side or direction **2** [C;U] morally just or legal claim

right³ adv **1** towards the right **2** correctly **3** exactly

rise¹ /raɪz/ v [I] **rose** /roz/, **risen** /ˈrɪzən/ **1** go up; get higher **2** (of the sun, etc.) come above the horizon

rise² n increase

risk /rɪsk/ n [C;U] chance that something bad may happen **at one's own risk** agreeing to bear any loss or danger **run/take a risk** do dangerous things ~**y** adj

roar /rɔr/ n deep loud continuing sound: roars of laughter ♦ v **1** v [I] give a roar **2** v [T] say forcefully

roll /rol/ v **1** [I/T] turn over and over or from side to side: The ball rolled into the hole. **2** vt form into esp. a tube by curling round and round **3** vi move steadily and smoothly (as if) on wheels

rope /rop/ n [C;U] (piece of) strong thick cord

rough /rʌf/ adj **1** having an uneven surface **2** stormy and violent: rough weather **3** lacking gentleness, good manners, or consideration: rough handling at the airport **4** (of food and living conditions) not delicate; simple **5** not detailed or exact: a rough estimate ~**ly** adv not exactly

round /raʊnd/ adj **1** circular **2** shaped like a ball

ru·mor /ˈrumər/ n [C;U] (piece of) information, perhaps untrue, spread from person to person ~**ed** adj reported unofficially

run /rʌn/ v **ran** /ræn/, **run**, pres. p. –**nn**– **1** v [I] (of people and animals) move faster than a walk **2** v [T] take part in (a race) by running **3** v [I/T] (cause to) move quickly: The car ran into a tree. **4** v [I/T] (cause to) work: This machine runs on/by electricity.

run out of phr v [T] use all of something: We've run out of gas.

rush /rʌʃ/ v **1** v [I/T] (cause to) go suddenly and quickly **2** v [I] hurry ♦ n [C] sudden rapid movement

safe¹ /sef/ adj out of danger

safe² n thick metal box with a lock, for keeping valuable things in

safe·ty /ˈsefti/ n [U] condition of being safe

said /sɛd/ past t. and p. of say

sal·a·ry /ˈsæləri/ n [C;U] fixed regular pay each month for a job, esp. for workers of higher rank ~**ried** adj receiving a salary

sale /sel/ n **1** [C;U] (act of) selling **2** [C] special offering of goods at low prices

sat·is·fac·to·ry /ˌsætɪsˈfæktəri/ adj **1** pleasing **2** good enough

sat·is·fy /ˈsætɪsfaɪ/ v [T] **1** please **2** fulfill (a need, desire, etc.) **3** fml fit (a condition, rule, standard, etc.) **4** persuade fully

saw·mill /ˈsɔmɪl/ n machine for cutting wood into pieces, or place where this is done

scar·y /ˈskɛəri/ adj frightening

scene /sin/ n **1** piece of action in one place in a play or film **2** background for action of a play: There are few scene changes. **3** place where something happens: the scene of the crime ~**ic** adj pleasant or impressive, esp. of nature

sched·ule /ˈskɛdʒul ‖ BrE ˈʃɛdʒəl/ n **1** planned list or order of things to be done **2** timetable of trains, buses, classes, etc. **3 ahead of/on/ behind schedule** before/at/after the planned or expected time ♦ v [T] plan for a certain future time

schol·ar·ship /ˈskɑlərˌʃɪp/ n **1** [C] payment so that someone can attend a college **2** [U] exact and serious study

scream /skrim/ v [I/T] **1** cry out in a loud high voice: (fig.) The wind screamed around the house. **2** draw attention, as if by such a cry ♦ n sudden loud cry

sea /si/ n **1** [the U] great body of salty water that covers much of the Earth's surface **2** [C] **a** particular (named) part of this: the Caribbean Sea **b** body of salt water (mostly) enclosed by land: the Mediterranean Sea

sea·way /ˈsiwe/ n **1** a sea route **2** a stretch of deep inland water for ships

see /si/ v **saw** /sɔ/, **seen** /sin/ **1** v [I] have or use the power of sight **2** v [T] notice, recognize, or examine by looking **3** v [I/T] come to know or understand: I can't see why you don't like it. **4** v [T] form an opinion or picture of in the mind: I see little hope of any improvement. **5** v [T] visit, meet, or receive as a visitor **6** v [I/T] (try to) find out: I'll see if he's there. **7** v [T] go with: I'll see you home. **8 (I'll) see you/be seeing you (soon/later/ next week, etc.)** (used when leaving a friend)

seem /sim/ v give the idea or effect of being; appear: She seems happy.

self-es·teem /ˌsɛlf-ɪˈstim/ n [U] one's good opinion of one's own worth

self·ish /ˈsɛlfɪʃ/ adj concerned with one's own advantage without care for others

sense /sɛns/ n **1** [C] intended meaning **2** [U] good and esp. practical understanding and judgment **3** [C] any of the five natural powers of sight, hearing, feeling, tasting, and smelling **sensible** adj showing good judgment

sen·si·tive /ˈsɛnsətɪv/ adj **1** quick to feel or show the effect of: sensitive to light **2** easily offended **3** (of an apparatus) measuring exactly

shake /ʃek/ v **shook** /ʃʊk/, **shaken** /ˈʃekən/ **1** v [I/T] move up and down and from side to side with quick short movements **2** v [I/T] hold (someone's right hand) and move it up and down, to show esp. greeting or agreement

she /ʃi/ pron (used for the female subject of a sentence)

shock /ʃɑk/ v expose to an unpleasant surprise ♦ n damage from electricity, being dropped, hit, etc. ~**proof** adj (esp. of a watch) not easily damaged by being dropped, hit, etc. ~**ed** adj unpleasantly surprised

shoe /ʃu/ n covering worn on the foot

shoot /ʃut/ v **shot** /ʃɑt/ **1** v [I] fire a weapon **2** v [T] (of a person or weapon) send out (bullets, etc.) with force **3** v [I] move very quickly or suddenly: The car shot past us.

should /ʃəd; strong ʃʊd/ v aux **1** ought to; will probably **2** (used after **that** in certain expressions of feeling): It's odd that you should mention him. (= The fact that you have mentioned him is odd.)

show up phr v [I] arrive; be present

shy /ʃaɪ/ adj nervous in the company of others

sight /saɪt/ n **1** [U] power of seeing **2** [S;U] the seeing of something

sign /saɪn/ n mark which represents a known meaning: + is the plus sign. ♦ v [I/T] write one's name to show that one is the writer

sign off phr v [I] end a TV or radio broadcast

sign on phr v [I/T] (cause to) join a working force by signing a paper

sign up phr v [I/T] (cause to) sign an agreement to take part in something or take a job

sig·nal /ˈsɪɡnəl/ n **1** sound or action which warns, commands, or gives a message: a danger signal **2** message sent by radio or television waves ♦ v [I] **–l–** give a signal

sil·ly /ˈsɪli/ adj not serious or sensible; foolish ~**liness** n [U]

sil·ver·ware /ˈsɪlvərˌwɛər/ n [U] forks, knives and spoons, even if they are not silver

sim·i·lar /ˈsɪmələr/ adj almost but not exactly the same; alike ~**ly** adv

skin·ny /ˈskɪni/ adj very thin

sleep /slip/ v [I] **slept** /slɛpt/ rest in natural unconscious resting state

sleeping bag /ˈslipɪŋ bæɡ/ n large warm bag for sleeping in

slow down /slo/ phr v [I/T] (to cause to) reduce speed

smash /smæʃ/ v **1** v [I/T] break into pieces violently **2** v [I/T] go, drive, hit forcefully: The car smashed into a lamppost. **3** v [T] hit (the ball) with a smash ♦ n (sound of) a violent breaking

smell /smɛl/ v **1** v [I] have or use the sense of the nose **2** v [T] notice, examine, etc., (as if) by this sense: I think I smell gas! ♦ n **1** [U] power of using the nose to discover the presence of gases in the air **2** [C] bad smell ~**y** adj smelling bad

smoke /smok/ n **1** [U] usu. white, grey, or black gas produced by burning **2** [S] act of smoking tobacco **smoky** adj filled with smoke **smoking** n [U] practice or habit of smoking cigarettes, etc.

snow /sno/ n [U] frozen rain that falls in white pieces and often forms a soft covering on the ground

so¹ /so/ adv **1** to such a (great) degree: It was so dark I couldn't see. **2** (used instead of repeating something): He hopes he'll win, and I hope so too. **3** also: He hopes he'll win, and so do I. **4** very: We're so glad you could come! **5 so far** up till now; up to this point

so² conj **1** with the result that: It was dark, so I couldn't see. **2** therefore: He had a headache, so he went to bed. **3** with the purpose (that): I gave him an apple, so (that) he wouldn't go hungry.

so·lar /ˈsolər/ adj of or from the sun

so·lu·tion /səˈluʃən/ n answer to a problem or question

soothe /suð/ v [T] **1** make less angry or excited **2** make less painful **soothing** adj **soothingly** adv

sound /saʊnd/ n **1** [C;U] what is or may be heard **2** [S] idea produced by something read or heard ♦ v **1** v [I] seem when heard: His explanation sounded suspicious. **2** v [I/T] (cause to) make a sound: Sound the trumpets. ~**proof** adj that sound cannot get through or into: a soundproof room

soup /sup/ n [U] liquid cooked food often containing pieces of meat or vegetables

source /sɔrs, sors/ n where something comes from; cause

south /saʊθ/ n (often cap.) the direction which is on the right of a person facing the rising sun

south·ern /ˈsʌðərn/ adj of the south part of the world or of a country ~**er** n (often cap.) person who lives in or comes from the southern part of a country

spe·cial /ˈspɛʃəl/ adj **1** of a particular kind; not ordinary **2** particularly great: a special occasion ♦ n something not of the regular kind

spin /spɪn/ v [I/T] **spun** /spʌn/, pres. p.

–nn– turn around and around fast ♦ n [S;U] fast turning movement

spoiled /spɔɪld/ adj treated very or too well

stand /stænd/ v **stood** /stʊd/ **1** v [I] support oneself on one's feet in an upright position **2** v [I] rise to a position of doing this: They stood (up) when he came in. **3** v [I/T] (cause to) rest in a position, esp. upright or on a base: the clock stood on the shelf. **4** v [T] like; bear: I can't stand (= don't like) whiskey.

start¹ /stɑrt/ v **1** v [I/T] begin **2** v [I/T] (cause to) come into existence: How did the trouble start? **3** v [I/T] (cause to) begin operation: The car won't start. **4** v [I] begin a journey

start² n beginning of an activity

state /steɪt/ n **1** [C] particular way of being; condition: the current state of our economy **2** [C;U] government or political organization of a country: industry controlled by the state **3** [C] area within a nation that governs itself: the states of the US

stat·ue /'stætʃu/ n (large) stone or metal likeness of a person, etc.

stay /steɪ/ v [I] **1** remain in a place rather than leave **2** continue to be; remain: trying to stay healthy **3** live in a place for a while: staying at a hotel

stay up phr v [I] **1** remain in an upright or higher position **2** stay out of bed

steal /stil/ v [I/T] **stole** /stoʊl/, **stolen** /'stoʊlən/ take (what belongs to someone else) without permission

still¹ /stɪl/ adv **1** (even) up to this/that moment: He's still here.

still² adj **1** not moving **2** without wind **3** silent; calm

stove /stoʊv/ n appliance that provides heat for cooking or warmth

strange /streɪndʒ/ adj **1** unusual; surprising **2** unfamiliar ~**er** n unknown person ~**ly** adv ~**ness** n [U]

strap /stræp/ n strong narrow band used as a fastening or support: a luggage strap ♦ v [T] –pp– fasten with straps

strap in phr v [I/T] strap

stress /stres/ n [C;U] **1** (worry resulting from) pressure caused by difficulties **2** degree of force put on a part of a word when spoken ♦ v [T] mention strongly

strike /straɪk/ v **struck** /strʌk/ **1** hit sharply **2** make a (sudden) attack **3** harm suddenly: They were struck down with illness.

strong /strɔŋ/ adj **1** having great power **2** not easily becoming broken, changed, destroyed, or ill **3** having a powerful effect on the mind or senses: a strong smell **4** (of a drink, drug, etc.) having a lot of the substance which gives taste, produces effect, etc.: This coffee is too strong.

stud·y /'stʌdi/ n **1** [U] also **studies** pl. —act of studying **2** [C] thorough

enquiry into a particular subject, esp. including a piece of writing on it **3** [C] room for working in; office ♦ v [I/T] spend time learning

sue /su/ v [I/T] bring a legal claim (against)

sug·ar /'ʃʊgər/ n [U] sweet white or brown plant substance used in food and drinks

sug·gest /səg'dʒest/ v [T] state as an idea for consideration: I suggest we do it this way. ~**ion** /səg'dʒestʃən/ n [C;U] act of suggesting or something suggested

su·i·cide /'suəsaɪd/ n [C;U] killing oneself

su·per·sti·tion /,supər'stɪʃən/ n [C;U] (unreasonable) belief based on old ideas about luck, magic, etc. ~**tious** adj

sure /ʃʊər/ adj **1** having no doubt **2** certain (to happen): You're sure to (=certainly will) like it. **3** confident (of having): I've never felt more sure of success. ~**ly** adv

sur·geon /'sɜrdʒən/ n doctor who does surgery

surgery /'sɜrdʒəri/ n [U] (performance of) medical operations: He was in surgery for five hours

sur·prise /sə'praɪz/ n [C;U] (feeling caused by) an unexpected event ♦ v [T] cause surprise to

sur·pris·ing /sər'praɪzɪŋ, sə'praɪ-/ adj unusual; causing surprise ~**ly** adv

sur·vive /sər'vaɪv/ v [I/T] continue to live or exist (after), esp. after coming close to death: She survived the accident. ~**vival** n [C] something which has survived from an earlier time ~**vivor** n

sus·pi·cious /sə'spɪʃəs/ adj **1** suspecting guilt, bad or criminal behavior, etc. **2** making one suspicious: suspicious behavior

swear /swear/ v **swore** /swɔr, swor/, **sworn** /swɔrn, sworn/ **1** v [I] curse **2** v [I/T] make a solemn promise or statement: She swore to tell the truth.

sweep /swip/ v **swept** /swept/ **1** v [T] clean or remove by brushing **2** v [I/T] move (over) or carry quickly and powerfully: A wave of panic swept over her.

sweet /swit/ adj **1** tasting like sugar **2** pleasing to the senses: sweet music **3** charming; lovable: What a sweet little boy!

take /teɪk/ v **took** /tʊk/, **taken** /'teɪkən/ **1** v [T] move from one place to another: Take the chair into the garden. **2** v [T] remove without permission: Someone's taken my pen. **3** v [T] subtract: What do you get if you take five from twelve? **4** v [T] get by performing an action: Take his temperature. | He took notes. | Take a seat. **5** v [T] start to hold: She took my arm. **6** v [T] use for travel: I take the train to work. **7** v [T] accept as true or worthy of attention: Take my advice. **8** v [T] need: The journey takes (= lasts) 2 hours. **9** v [T] do; perform: He took

a walk/a bath. **10** v [T] put into the body: take some medicine/a deep breath **11** v [T] make by photography **12 take care of** look after **13 take it easy** infml relax

take away phr v [T] remove; subtract

talk /tɔk/ v [I] speak: Can the baby talk yet? | Is there somewhere quiet where we can talk?

talk about phr v [T] discuss

tank /tæŋk/ n **1** large liquid or gas container **2** enclosed armored military vehicle with a large gun

taste /teɪst/ n **1** [C;U] quality by which a food or drink is recognized in the mouth: Sugar has a sweet taste. **2** [U] sense which recognizes food or drink as sweet, salty, etc. ♦ v [I] have a particular taste: These oranges taste nice.

tax /tæks/ n [C;U] money which must be paid to the government

teach /titʃ/ v [I/T] **taught** /tɔt/ give knowledge or skill of (something) to (someone): He taught me French. ~**er** n person who teaches, esp. as a job ~**ing** n [U] **1** job of a teacher **2** also **teachings** pl. —moral beliefs taught by someone of historical importance: the teachings of Christ

teen·ag·er /'tin,eɪdʒər/ n person of between thirteen and nineteen years old; adolescent **teenage** adj

tel·e·phone /'telə,foʊn/ n [C;U] (apparatus for) the sending and receiving of sounds over long distances by electric means ♦ v [I/T] (try to) speak (to) by telephone

tell /tel/ v **told** /toʊld/ **1** v [T] make (something) known to (someone) in words: Are you telling me the truth? | Tell me how to do it. **2** v [T] warn; advise: I told you it wouldn't work. **3** v [T] order: I told him to do it. **4 tell the time** read the time from a watch or clock

tem·pe·ra·ture /'tempərətʃər/ n **1** [C;U] degree of heat or coldness: the average temperature **2** [S] body temperature higher than the correct one; fever

tent /tent/ n cloth shelter supported usu. by poles and ropes, used esp. by campers

ter·ri·fy /'terə,faɪ/ v [T] frighten extremely: His expression terrified me. **terrified** adj **terrifying** adj

ter·ror /'terər/ n [U] extreme fear

the·at·er /'θiətər/ n (building) where plays are performed

their /ðeər; weak ðər/ det of them: their house

then /ðen/ adv **1** at that time: I was happier then. **2** next; afterwards: . . . and then we went home. **3** in that case: Have you finished? Then you can watch TV.

the·o·ry /'θiəri/ n statement intended to explain a fact or event

ther·a·py /'θerəpi/ n [C;U] treatment of illnesses of the body or mind ~**pist** n

there¹ /ðeər/ adv **1** at or to that place:

He lives over there. **2** (used for drawing attention to someone or something): There goes John.

there² pron (used for showing that something or someone exists or happens, usu. as the subject of **be**, **seem to be**, or **appear to be**): There's someone at the door.

thief /θif/ n **thieves** /θivz/ person who steals

think /θɪŋk/ v **thought** /θɔt/ **1** v [I] use the mind to make judgments **2** v [T] have as an opinion; believe: Do you think it will rain? **3** v [T] have as a plan.

thought¹ /θɔt/ past t. and p. of think

thought² n **1** [C] something thought; idea, etc. **2** [U] thinking **3** [U] serious consideration ~**less** adj showing a selfish or careless lack of thought ~**lessly** adv

thrill /θrɪl/ n (something producing) a sudden strong feeling of excitement, fear, etc. ♦ v [I/T] (cause to) feel a thrill ~**er** n book, film, etc., telling a very exciting (crime) story ~**ing** adj

throw /θroʊ/ v **threw** /θru/, **thrown** /θroʊn/ **1** v [I/T] send (something) through the air with a sudden movement of the arm **2** v [T] move or put forcefully or quickly: The two fighters threw themselves at each other. **3** v [T] cause to fall to the ground: Her horse threw her. **4** v [T] make one's voice appear to come from somewhere other than one's mouth

throw away/out phr v [T] get rid of

tie /taɪ/ v [T] **tied**; pres. p. **tying 1** v [I/T] fasten by knotting: tie a parcel/one's shoe laces **2** make (a knot) for this purpose

tire¹ /taɪər/ v [I/T] (cause to) become tired ~**ing** adj ~**less** adj never getting tired ~**some** adj **1** annoying **2** uninteresting

tire² n thick band of rubber around the outside edge of a wheel

tired /taɪərd/ adj **1** needing rest or sleep **2** no longer interested: I'm tired of doing this; let's go for a walk. **3** showing lack of imagination or new thought: tired ideas ~**ness** n [U]

to /tə; before vowels tʊ; strong tu/ prep **1** in a direction towards: the road to Fredonia **2 a** (used before a verb to show it is the infinitive): I want to go. **b** used in place of infinitive: We didn't want to come but we had to. **3** so as to be in: I was sent to prison. **4** touching: Stick the paper to the wall. **5** as far as: from beginning to end **6** for the attention or possession of: I told/gave it to her. **7** in connection with: the answer to a question **8** (of time) before: It's ten to four.

too /tu/ adv **1** to a greater degree than is necessary or good: You're driving too fast. **2** also: I've been to Montreal, and to Quebec too.

tough /tʌf/ adj **1** not easily weakened or broken **2** difficult to cut or eat:

tough meat **3** difficult: *a tough job/problem* **4** not kind, severe: *a tough new law*

tour /tʊər/ *n* act of traveling or walking around somewhere to look at interesting things ♦ *v* [I/T] visit as a tourist ~**ism** *n* [U] ~**ist** *n*

trav·el /'trævəl/ *v* –**l**– **1** *v* [I/T] make a journey (through) **2** *v* [T] cover (the stated distance) on a journey **3** *v* [I] go, pass, move, etc.: *At what speed does light travel?* ~**er** *n* person on a journey

trick /trɪk/ *n* **1** clever act or plan to deceive or cheat someone **2** amusing or confusing skillful act: *magic/card tricks*

troub·le /'trʌbəl/ *n* **1** [C;U] (cause of) difficulty, worry, annoyance, etc.: *I didn't have any trouble doing it; it was easy.* **2** [U] state of being blamed: *He's always getting into trouble with the police.* **3** [S;U] inconvenience or more than usual work or effort: *I took a lot of trouble to get it right.*

trust·ful /'trʌstfʊl/ *adj* (too) ready to trust others

truth /truθ/ *n* **truths** /truðz, truθs/ **1** [C,U] that which is true: *Are you telling the truth?* **2** [C] true fact

try /traɪ/ *v* **1** *v* [I/T +to-v] make an attempt: *I tried to persuade him, but failed.* **2** *v* [T] test by use and experience: *Have you tried this new soap?*

turn¹ /tɜrn/ *v* **1** *v* [I/T] move around a central point: *The wheels turned.* **2** *v* [I/T] move so that a different side faces upwards or outwards: *She turned the pages.* **3** *v* [I] change direction: *Turn right at the end of the road.* **4** *v* [T] go around: *The car turned the corner.* **5** *v* [I] look around: *She turned to wave.* **6** *v* [I/T] (cause to) become: *His hair has turned gray.*

turn around *phr v* [I/T] (cause to) face the opposite direction

turn into *phr v* [T] (cause to) become something else: *The witch turned the prince into a frog. The caterpillar turned into a butterfly.*

turn off *phr v* [T] stop the flow or operation of: *turn off the tap/television*

turn out *phr v* **1** *v* [T] stop the operation of (a light) **2** *v* [T] drive out; send away **3** *v* [I] come out or gather (as if) for a meeting or public event **4** *v* [T] produce: *The factory turns out 100 cars a day.* **5** happen to be in the end: *The party turned out a success.*

turn over *phr v* [I/T] (cause to) have the opposite side facing upwards

turn² *n* **1** act of turning (something) **2** change of direction **3** rightful chance or duty to do something: *It's my turn to speak.*

tur·tle /'tɜrtl/ *n* (sea) animal with four legs and a hard curved shell

type /taɪp/ *n* **1** [C] sort; kind; example of a group or class: *She's just that type of person.* **2** [U] printed letters: *italic type* ♦ *v* [I/T] write with a type-writer or word processor

ul·ti·mate /ˈʌltəmɪt/ *adj* **1** *infml* greatest or best: *the ultimate bicycle* **2** after all others: *our ultimate destination* ♦ ~**ly** *adv* finally

un·be·liev·a·ble /ʌnbɪˈlivəbəl/ *adj* very surprising: *It's unbelievable how many children she has!*

un·com·for·ta·ble /ʌnˈkʌmfərtəbəl/ *adj* **1** not comfortable **2** embarrassed ~**bly** *adv*

un·com·mon /ʌnˈkɑmən/ *adj* not common

un·con·scious /ʌnˈkɑnʃəs/ *adj* **1** having lost consciousness **2** not intentional

un·count·a·ble /ʌnˈkaʊntəbəl/ *adj* that cannot be counted: *'Furniture' is an uncountable noun —You can't say 'two furnitures'.*

un·der·stand /ʌndərˈstænd/ *v* –**stood** /-ˈstʊd/ **1** *v* [I/T] know or find the meaning (of): *She spoke in Russian, and I didn't understand.* **2** *v* [T] know or feel closely the nature of (a person, feelings, etc.) ~**able** *adj* ~**ing** *n* [U] mental power; ability to understand

un·der·wa·ter /ˌʌndərˈwɔtər/ *adj, adv* below the surface of the water

un·do /ʌnˈdu/ *v* [T] –**did** /-ˈdɪd/, –**done** /-ˈdʌn/ **1** unfasten (something tied or wrapped) **2** remove the effects of: *The fire undid months of hard work.*

un·faith·ful /ʌnˈfeθfəl/ *adj* having sex with someone other than one's regular partner

unfortunate /ʌnˈfɔrtʃənɪt/ *adj* **1** that makes one sorry **2** unlucky ~**ly** *adv*

u·ni·form /ˈyunəfɔrm/ *n* sort of clothes worn by all members of a group: *nurse's/army uniform*

un·in·ter·est·ed /ʌnˈɪntrɪstɪd/ *adj* not interested

u·ni·ted /yuˈnaɪtɪd/ *adj* **1** joined **2** having become one **3** acting together for a purpose

un·known /ʌnˈnon/ *adj* not able to be recognised; not familiar

un·luck·y /ʌnˈlʌki/ *adj* not lucky

un·nat·u·ral /ʌnˈnætʃərəl/ *adj* **1** unusual **2** against ordinary good ways of behaving: *unnatural sexual practices*

un·pack /ʌnˈpæk/ *v* [I/T] remove (possessions) from (a container)

un·pleas·ant /ʌnˈplɛzənt/ *adj* **1** not enjoyable **2** unkind

un·self·ish /ʌnˈselfɪʃ/ *adj* not concerned with one's own advantage, but caring more for others

un·u·su·al /ʌnˈyuʒuəl, -ʒəl/ *adj fml* **1** not common **2** interesting because different from others ~**ly** *adv* **1** very **2** in an unusual way

up·set /ʌpˈsɛt/ *v* [T] –**set**; *pres. p.* –**tt**– **1** turn over, esp. accidentally, causing confusion or scattering **2** cause to be worried, sad, etc.

u·su·al /ˈyuʒuəl/ *adj* in accordance with what happens most of the time: *He lacked his usual cheerfulness.* ~**ly** *adv*

va·can·cy /ˈvekənsi/ *n* unfilled place, such as a job or hotel room

vac·u·um /ˈvækyum/ *v* [T] clean with a vacuum cleaner

var·i·ous /ˈvɛəriəs/ *adj* several: *There are various ways of going.* ~**ly** *adv*

vege·ta·ble /ˈvɛdʒtəbəl/ *n* (non-sweet edible part of) plant

ven·tril·o·quist /vɛnˈtrɪləkwɪst/ *n* someone who can make their voice seem to come from somewhere else ~**quism** *n* [U]

vet·e·ri·na·ri·an /ˌvɛtərəˈnɛriən, ˌvɛtrə-/ *n* animal doctor

vil·lage /ˈvɪlɪdʒ/ *n* small collection of houses in a country area ~**lager** *n* person who lives in a village

vote /vot/ *v* [I] express one's choice officially, esp. by marking a piece of paper or raising one's hand ♦ *n* [C;U] (choice made by) voting

wake /wek/ *v* [I/T] **woke** /wok/, **waked** or **woken** /ˈwokən/ (cause to) stop sleeping: *I woke up late.*

want /wɑnt/ *v* [I/T +to-v] **1** have a strong desire for: *I don't want to go.* **2** wish for the presence of: *Your mother wants you.*

ward·robe /ˈwɔrdrob/ *n* **1** large cupboard for clothes **2** person's collection of clothes

warn·ing /ˈwɔrnɪŋ/ *n* [C;U] **1** telling in advance: *They attacked without warning.* **2** something that tells of something bad that may happen, or how to prevent it: *That's the second warning we've had.*

wa·ter·proof /ˈwɔtərˌpruf/ *adj, n* not allowing water (rain) through or into ♦ *v* [T] make waterproof

wave /wev/ *v* **1** *v* [I/T] move (one's hand or something in it) as a signal: *We waved as the train pulled out.* **2** *v* [T] direct with a movement of the hand: *The policeman waved the traffic on.* ♦ *n* **1** form in which light, sound, etc., move: *radio waves* **2** raised moving area of water (on the sea)

way /we/ *n* **1** [C] road, path, etc., to follow in order to reach a place: *She asked me the way to the station. | We lost our way.* **2** [C] direction: *He went that way.* **3** [S] distance: *We're a long way from home.* **4** [C] method: *Do it this way.* **5** **by the way** (used to introduce a new subject in speech)

wear /wɛər/ *v* **wore** /wɔr/, **worn** /wɔrn/ *v* [T] have (esp. clothes) on the body ♦ *n* [U] **1** clothes: *evening wear | men's wear* **2** act of wearing esp. clothes

weath·er /ˈwɛðər/ *n* [U] particular condition of wind, sunshine, rain, snow, etc.: *a day of fine weather* **under the weather** slightly ill

wed·ding /ˈwɛdɪŋ/ *n* marriage ceremony

weigh /we/ *v* **1** *v* [T] find the weight of: *weigh oneself* **2** *v* [I] have the stated weight: *It weighs six lbs.*

well¹ *adv* **better** /ˈbɛtər/, **best** /bɛst/ in a good way: *She sings well.*

well² *n* **1** place where fluid can be taken from underground

when /wɛn/ *adv, conj* at what time; at the time that: *When will they come? | He looked up when she came in.*

where /wɛər/ *adv, conj* at or to a place: *Where do you live? | Sit where you like.*

wheth·er /ˈwɛðər/ *conj* if ... or not: *I'm trying to decide whether to go.*

while /waɪl/ *n* [S] **1** length of time: *He's been gone quite a while.* (= a fairly long time) **2** **once in a while** sometimes, but not often ♦ *conj* during the time that: *They arrived while we were having dinner.*

who /hu/ *pro* what person

whole /hol/ *adj* all; complete: *I spent the whole day in bed.*

wid·ow /ˈwɪdo/ *n* woman whose husband has died ~**er** *n* man whose wife has died ~**ed** *adj*

will /wɪl/ *v aux, neg* **won't 1** (expresses the future tense): *Will it rain tomorrow?* **2** be willing to: *I won't go!* **3** (used in requests): *Will you shut the door?*

win /wɪn/ *v* [I/T] **won** /wʌn/, *pres. p.* –**nn**– be first or best (in) beating one's opponent(s): *Who won the race?* ~**nings** *n* [P] money won

wom·an /ˈwʊmən/ *n* **women** /ˈwɪmɪn/ **1** adult female person **2** women in general

won·der /ˈwʌndər/ *n* [U] feeling of strangeness, surprise, and usu. admiration ♦ *v* [I] wish to know

wood /wʊd/ *n* **1** [U] substance of which trees are made **2** [C] place where trees grow, smaller than a forest ~**en** *adj* made of wood

work /wɜrk/ *n* [U] **1** activity done to produce something or gain a result **2** job; business: *I go to work by train.* ♦ *v* [I] **1** do an activity which uses effort, esp. as one's job: *She works at the factory.* **2** (of a machine, plan, etc.) operate (properly): *It works by electricity. | Your plan will never work.*

work out *phr v* [T] **1** calculate/find (the answer to) **2** exercise

would /d, əd, wəd; *strong* wʊd/ *v aux* **1** (past of **will**): *They said they would meet us at 10:30.* **2** (shows what is likely or possible): *What would you do if you won a million dollars?* **3** (shows choice): *I'd rather have eggs.* **4** (expressing a polite request): *Would you lend me your pencil?*

wound¹ /wund/ *n* damaged place on the body, esp. caused by a weapon: *a bullet wound* ♦ *v* [T] cause a wound to

wound² /waʊnd/ *v* past tense and past participle of wind /waɪnd/

yet /yɛt/ *adv* up until this time: *He hasn't arrived yet.*

yo·gurt /ˈyogərt/ *n* [U] milk that has thickened and turned slightly acid through the action of certain healthy bacteria

your /yər; *strong* yʊər, yɔr, yor/ *det* of you: *your house*

you're /yər; *strong* yʊər, yɔr, yor/ *short for:* you are

zoo /zu/ *n* **zoos** park where many types of wild animal are kept for show

Grammar Review

Verbs
to be

simple present

I	am ('m)/ am not ('m not)	
You We They	are ('re)/ are not (aren't/'re not)	here now.
He She It	is ('s)/ is not (isn't/'s not)	

simple past

I He She It	was/ was not (wasn't)	here yesterday.
You We They	were/ were not (weren't)	

yes/no questions:
put the verb before the subject

Are they here now?	Yes, they **are**./ No, they**'re not**.
Was she here yesterday?	Yes, she **was**./ No, she **wasn't**.

wh- questions:
add the question word at the start of the question

What **are** they?	They're insects.
When **were** we there?	We were there yesterday.
Where **is** she?	She's in the kitchen.
Who **are** they?	They're my parents.
Why **was** he here?	He was here to visit us.
How **am** I?	I'm fine.

other verbs

simple present

I You We They	work/ do not (don't) work.	
He She It	works/ does not (doesn't) work.	

simple past (see irregular verbs list)

I You He She It We They	worked/ did not (didn't) work.	yesterday.

yes/no questions:
put **do** before the subject, change the verb to the bare infinitive form

Do they **work**?	Yes, they **do**./ No, they **don't**.
Does she **work**?	Yes, she **does**./ No, she **doesn't**.
Did he **work** yesterday?	Yes, he **did**./ No, he **didn't**.

wh- questions:
add the question word at the start of the question.

What **do** they **do**?	They study.
When **did** we **leave**?	We left yesterday.
Where **does** she **work**?	She works at the University.
Who **do** they **know**?	They know my brother.
Why **did** he **work**?	He needed some money.
How **do** you **know** her?	She's in my class.

present continuous

I	**am ('m)/** **am not ('m not)**		
You We They	**are ('re)/** **are not (aren't/'re not)**	**working.**	
He She It	**is ('s)/** **is not (isn't/'s not)**		

past continuous

I He She It	**was/** **was not (wasn't)**	**working.**
You We They	**were /** **were not (weren't)**	

present perfect (see irregular verbs list)

I You We They	**have ('ve)/** **have not (haven't)**	**worked.**
He She It	**has ('s)** **has not (hasn't)**	

yes/no questions:
put *be/have* before the subject

Are you
  working?
	Yes, we **are.**/
	  No, we **aren't.**

Were they
  working?
	Yes, they **were.**/
	  No, they **weren't.**

Has it **worked?**	Yes, it **has.**/ No, it **hasn't.**

wh- questions:
add the question word at the start of the question.

What **are** we **doing?**	We're working.
When **were** they **working?**	They were working yesterday.
Where **has** she **worked?**	She's worked at the University.
Who **have** I **seen** already?	I've seen my brother.
Why **was** he **studying?**	He needed a good grade.
How **is** she **doing?**	She's doing fine.

Reported Speech

direct			reported
"I'm tired,"			was tired.
"I work too much,"			worked too much.
"I'm quitting my job,"			was quitting his job.
"I wasn't happy,"	he said.	He said	hadn't been happy.
"I returned to school,"		(that) he	had returned to school.
"I wasn't studying enough,"			hadn't been studying enough.
"I've been much happier,"			had been much happier.
"Are you tired?"			I was tired.
"Was she happy?"			she had been happy.
"Do you work?"	she asked.	She asked	I worked.
"Did she leave?"		if/ whether	she had left.
"Have we finished?"			we had finished.